‘You’re
going to

‘Why? So y … into the dust for the second time. You don’t know anything about loving, Ross, unless it’s when you’re looking in the mirror.’

‘You could teach me,’ he offered unabashed. ‘I might enjoy that.’

‘I’m sure you won’t be short of offers.’

Dear Reader

Well, summer is almost upon us. Time to think about holidays, perhaps? Where to go? What to do? And how to get everything you own into one suitcase! Wherever you decide to go, don't forget to pack plenty of Mills & Boon novels. This month's selection includes such exotic locations as Andalucía, Brazil and the Aegean Islands, so you can enjoy lots of holiday romance even if you stay at home!

The Editor

Christine Greig works full-time as a senior marketing manager in the communications industry. This involves a great deal of travel, both within Europe and the United States, which she enjoys very much. She has a BA Hons degree and a diploma in marketing. She is in her thirties, came originally from North Yorkshire, England, and is married.

PASSIONATE OBSESSION

BY

CHRISTINE GREIG

MILLS & BOON

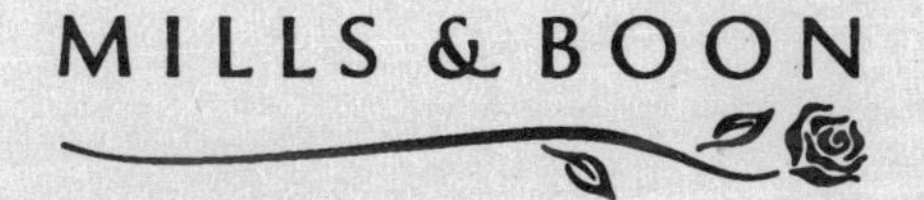

MILLS & BOON LIMITED
ETON HOUSE, 18-24 PARADISE ROAD
RICHMOND, SURREY TW9 1SR

First published in Great Britain 1994
by Mills & Boon Limited

This edition 1994

ISBN 0 263 78512 2

Set in Times Roman 10 on 11½ pt.
01-9406-52869 C

Made and printed in Great Britain

CHAPTER ONE

RAIN streamed down the windows of the gatehouse mixed with sleet, the wind buffeting the panes making them rattle in the frames. Scarlett looked out towards Saxonbridge Farm, its brightly lit warmth suggesting that she and Jordan were not totally alone in the world.

Going into the small front room, Scarlett blinked as headlights from the road reflected from wall to wall. It was going to be a stormy night. Beyond the wind was the pounding sea, a dull boom as the sea climbed and clawed at the ever-eroding cliff.

Putting the light on, Scarlett flinched as a dark shape appeared to move outside. It must be a trick of light. No one would be out on such a night. Closing the curtains, she tensed as the doorbell rang. It was only half-past eight in the evening but she felt disinclined to open the door. The bell rang again and she heard a growled, 'Come on—are you deaf?' before the wood bounced under the beat of a fist.

'Yes?' Her voice sounded high and frightened. 'Who is it?'

'I'm looking for Saxonbridge Farm. I've missed the turning—— Look, lady, I'm getting drenched out here.'

'Saxonbridge Farm. Yes, carry on down the road,' she shouted back. The voice sounded familiar but she couldn't place it.

'What?' The wind howled with renewed ferocity, robbing the muffled explanations she was giving of any sense.

Scarlett put the chain on, glancing at the stout walking stick her father-in-law had left in the hall stand. Opening the door, she prepared to repeat the message.

The light spread out like a wave from the house, illuminating the porch, the swarthy features of the man coming into focus.

Scarlett froze on the spot, an icy cold surge of emotion shooting up from her toes.

'Ross——' Her choked cry was the only word she uttered, before the light was sucked away and she collapsed in the doorway.

The heavy thump of feet upstairs preceded the appearance of a young boy, who hesitated on his way down the stairs, spying his mother lying on the floor.

The man tried to push the door further open and then spied the child, seeing a viable alternative to snapping the chain.

'Can you let me in? I want to check your mother's OK. What's your name?' He became aware of the child's troubled features.

'Jordan.' The boy had black hair and near-black eyes and had a stubborn look about him.

'Well, Jordan, your mummy has fainted. She'll be all right soon but I think it would be better if I made sure she's all right.'

'Are you a doctor?'

The man paused, then said, 'I know first aid; that's like a doctor.' He felt disinclined to lie.

'I'm not supposed to speak to strangers. I'll phone Grandad. He's up at the farm.'

'Saxonbridge Farm?'

The boy nodded, eyeing him warily and picking up the phone. He dialled a number, quite impressive in his control of the situation. The conversation was brief; 'the man' was mentioned and no doubt galvanised activity at the other end of the line. Watching the woman breathe, he tried to ascertain her state of health. He didn't think she'd banged her head. He wondered where her husband was. He found the idea of the man of the house unwelcome. Something about the woman appealed to him. It nagged at him, a sense of...

The engine of a vehicle roared along the track from the farm. Seeing the lights, the stranger waited with a feeling of sick excitement. Would they welcome him or would he find this snippet of his past a source of disappointment—hostility even?

Mud squirted from beneath the tyres as the Land Rover skidded to a halt. Two men jumped out, one holding a shotgun. The stranger put his hands up, mocking the Wild West overtones but knowing enough of guns not to want to spook anybody.

The two men approached warily, rain running down their clothes. They hadn't paused to don waterproofs.

'I'm sorry to cause such a——' The words dried up in his throat, his gaze moving from one to the other. 'Is there something wrong?'

The elder man pushed him back into the light, staring into his face.

'Ross! Ross!' The words shook and he was caught up in a bear-hug with the younger man exclaiming incredulously and joining in the celebrations.

The boy opened the door and tugged at his grandfather's trousers.

'Grandad! Come and help Mum. I can't wake her up.'

Scarlett's eyes fluttered, her son's impassioned tones penetrating the fog that clouded her mind. Jordan crouched down beside her, patting her cheek as the men remembered their task and turned quickly to view the barely conscious woman.

'She fainted,' the stranger explained, confused.

'She would, lad!' the older man exclaimed. 'You've been gone six long years; didn't you expect it to be a shock?'

Frowning, he couldn't quite take it in. Ross, they called him. Ever since the accident, he had thought of himself as Chad Mathews. That hadn't been his name, he had discovered later, but it was the only one he had.

'I can't remember,' he exclaimed, automatically kneeling beside the woman. 'Let's get her somewhere comfortable—then we can talk.'

'I'll phone Mary.' The older man shook his head, beaming broadly. 'She'll run here in bare feet.'

'Mary?' He was beginning to feel overwhelmed. He guessed he had found part of his past but couldn't quite work out where he fitted in.

'Mum.' David, the younger man, squeezed his shoulder. 'What do you mean you can't remember? You must remember us, Mum, Dad, me?'

Dark eyes returned his eager gaze blankly.

'Not even Scarlett?'

'Scarlett?'

'Your wife.'

The door slammed shut with the wind, closing out the dark possibilties of the storm-ravaged night. Inside the house, the stranger's past rushed up to greet him with the overwhelming strength of the spring tide. He had a place. A past and a place to belong. Fitting back into that past brought a host of complexities that had yet to be appreciated. When the woman Scarlett focused dazedly on him, he realised it wasn't going to be easy. Her eyes were bewildered but in their topaz depths was an unmistakable glint of accusation.

The evening was a mixture of celebration and revelation for the McQuillans. Scarlett nursed a brandy, her eyes averted from the dark profile of her long-lost husband. That his glance touched her several times with open curiosity she was perfectly aware, but she was besieged by conflicting emotions. Mary McQuillan had her son back and for her life had never been sweeter but Scarlett hadn't forgotten; she had the past firmly and ingloriously intact. Ross had gone to Brazil on a rescue mission for a journalist friend, Joanne Williams. She had disappeared while investigating the conflict between the growing commercial concerns and the Indians who inhabited the rainforest. The fact that Scarlett had been struggling to acclimatise to the demands their baby son made on her had seemed to count for nothing.

It hadn't helped that the journalist was female, glamorous and Ross's ex-girlfriend. When Ross's helicopter had gone down on the return flight to the Brazilian city of Belém, Joanne Williams had very publicly led prayers for his safety. As far as the Press were concerned a young nobody, private in her grief, came a poor second in the publicity stakes to Joanne's tragic and very accessible feelings of loss. Scarlett had felt strangely unreal throughout the whole episode and it was only with maturity that she realised she had merely been playing a game as his wife. They had never had a true marriage. It had taken six years for her to heal the wounds of her first love and now Ross had come back, the past a blank except for a few dim memories, and she didn't know how to deal with the situation.

She had grown used to being a sole parent. Jordan had the right to get to know Ross but the idea of another McQuillan influencing her son was bad enough; the fact that he had significantly more rights than her in-laws disturbed her deeply.

Scarlett had been only seventeen when she'd fallen pregnant, and her hasty marriage to the older, infinitely more sophisticated Ross McQuillan had made right an episode of monumental folly on both their parts.

Scarlett was Mary McQuillan's god-daughter and had come to live with the McQuillans when her own parents had followed their calling providing medical assistance to Third World countries they considered in more need than their teenage daughter.

Ross was ten years older, an investigative journalist who had turned his skill with the written word into a goldmine writing political thrillers. His books were still popular, several having been made into films. His lifestyle had been a compromise between wandering the world for exotic locations and expanding the family's farming interests in North Yorkshire. Marriage had been the last thing on his agenda. Scarlett's youthful sensuality had homed in on his sexual magnetism, a world-shattering crush making her uncaring of the consequences.

Ross had seemed immune to her adoration until desperation had made her seek from him the emotional warmth lacking from her young life. He had considered their lovemaking a moment of passionate insanity, not to be repeated. His arguments had been predictable enough. She was too young for serious committment. If anyone found out about their brief affair, she would have to leave Saxonbridge. His lifestyle made a steady relationship almost impossible.

All of which left her feeling hurt and betrayed. When Scarlett had found out she was pregnant and Ross had dutifully made recompense, she'd had an uphill struggle believing he cared for her at all. True, he had shown tender concern for her 'delicate condition' and during the six months left of her pregnancy he had been all a husband should be. He had appeared to anticipate fatherhood with proud expectation, celebrating his young son when he was born with a masculine enthusiasm that had made her smile. She had begun to relax and believe their relationship could work. Ross had made her feel everything was possible when she lay in his arms, their lovemaking fierce and intense, taking them both to the very heights of ecstasy. A fragile sense of contentment had existed between them, their young son and a deep affection for Yorkshire providing common ground for something more enduring than physical attraction. Only the constant dinner invitations from his media colleagues and old university friends had brought back feelings of deep insecurity.

Then Joanne Williams had scored her final triumph. The news of her disappearance was on national news; so, too, the open speculation that without her more experienced partner Joanne had wandered into a volatile trouble spot without necessary back-up.

Ross had been on the phone within minutes. He had been astounded at Scarlett's reaction when she'd refused to hear of his going. Joanne, he had pointed out coldly, was being held by a group of desperate men, some of whom had few scruples about rape or murder. It was his territory, he knew whom to contact, his conscience would never let him rest if he let anything happen to his colleague because his wife was having a tantrum. Joanne's parents, old friends of the family, had added their pleas and events had moved swiftly after that.

Ross had left without her blessing. He had found Joanne, delivered her to safety, then gone missing on his way back, presumed a victim of engine malfunction. The helicopter wreckage had been found, the body of the pilot discovered a short distance away. The search party could find no sign of Ross and he was presumed to have died in the jungle. Scarlett had agonised over their parting, hated herself for her lack of generosity, her meanness of spirit. Joanne Williams had twisted the knife even deeper. Scarlett had run through every nameable emotion and a few more on Ross McQuillan's behalf and considered herself a burnt-out case.

Steeling herself, she dared a glance at Ross. She could recall his face easily. It was hard to forget with her child a living reminder and the shrine Mary McQuillan had made of the house. But the desperate love that had seared her seemed to have evaporated with her adolescence. If only at seventeen she had had the wisdom she now possessed.

Emboldened, she indulged her curiosity. He was still good-looking, she admitted grudgingly. Sun-bronzed skin enhanced his dark colouring, and his impressive self-assurance, even in the present circumstances, was like a wall protecting his emotions. She had been a moth to a flame, singeing herself trying to get close. Now she knew her limits. Ross McQuillan was not her type and never would be.

'I guess I must have wandered away from the crash,' he recollected, rubbing his fingers over his forehead. 'I don't remember that either, just searching my pockets and finding papers saying I was Chad Mathews. It turned out Chad Mathews was some cheap American crook. Fortunately for me, he was caught red-handed robbing a local store and I avoided picking up the tab for his crimes. He must have gone through my pockets when I was unconscious and had ideas about changing identities. I asked the police when I found out about Mathews but they weren't very helpful. I knew I wasn't Chad but that was all I knew.'

'It sounds like one of your books.' The words just popped out and Scarlett was aware of the family's censure.

Ross merely turned his attention on her, which was punishment enough. 'I have no reason to make it up.' Eyes black in the subdued lighting challenged her veiled criticism.

'Of course you haven't.' Mary McQuillan hugged his arm from her position beside him on the couch. 'I expect Scarlett is still recovering from the shock.'

Too true, Scarlett thought with a little flicker of anger sparking inside her. He was still the same! He might have forgotten the past but he hadn't had a personality transplant. Ross had a habit of putting people on the spot; he called a spade a spade and expected everyone else to do the same.

'What books?' he enquired as an afterthought. 'In Brazil I run a leisure business. I imagined I'd be in the same kind of work; I found it easy enough to run a business once I had an initial stake.'

His family filled in his past as far as they could and David plucked one of his books from the bookcase. Ross seemed genuinely fascinated. 'Funny, I've always kept a diary but, working with another language, I never took it further than that.'

Upstairs the thud of feet going towards the bathroom drew his attention.

'I suppose it's too late to——'

'Yes,' Scarlett interposed hurriedly. 'I'd rather you met Jordan when I've had a chance to explain. It's going to come as something of a shock.'

'Oh, but a nice one.' Mary McQuillan was all joy. 'Jordan's so missed having a father. Scarlett has done her best, of course, but it's not the same, is it?'

'It will take a while,' Ross agreed, eyeing Scarlett with a measure of caution. 'It's something we'll have to discuss. I haven't come to savage your young, Scarlett; you can sheathe your claws.'

'It's clear you'll have several decisions to make.' She knew practicality would be the last thing on the McQuillans' minds. 'If you're just here for a visit, I don't want Jordan's expectations raised just to dash them.'

'I can understand that.' Ross regarded her steadily. 'We need to talk. I can't be quite as sensible as you; this is all new for me. Finding out where I belong in the world is a relief that you probably can't imagine.'

'No,' she agreed, lowering her lashes, resenting the subdued criticism. 'I don't expect you to make any snap decisions.'

'Ross is home.' Mary McQuillan dismissed her daughter-in-law's reservations. 'He won't want to go back to that awful place. He has a life here, waiting for him.'

Ross smiled at his mother but his eyes returned to Scarlett. Being a son and a brother was fact and unchangeable; being a husband and a father was something else again. The woman knew that and she was arming herself for battle. Why he didn't know, but the gauntlet was down between them.

Scarlett endured the rest of the evening. She was conscious of Ross McQuillan's probing intelligence. He had weighed up the level of silent antipathy directed towards him and no doubt would return for their next meeting with his past history collected and thoroughly researched.

Clearing up the glasses left from their impromptu party, she let the memories free from their cobwebs. She hadn't really liked Ross at first. When she had come to live with the McQuillans he had just finished university and had got his first job in Fleet Street. He'd been full of himself and quite unbearable, she remembered. It had been David who had welcomed her into the family. Ross's brother had always been her friend but kind people rarely captured the imagination of young, silly girls.

She had well and truly upset the McQuillan applecart and been taken on as an irresponsible responsibility. Despite coping with Jordan, in the family's eyes she was still seventeen and still guilty of wrecking Ross's chances of a match worthy of his own brilliance. She had moved to the gatehouse to escape Mary McQuillan's censure and refusal to accept that she, Scarlett, was in charge of her child's future. The gatehouse was small. The loft had been converted and made into a bedroom for Jordan, only one bedroom and a bathroom being available on the upper floor, below a small dining-room, parlour and kitchen.

It was a nice house and they fitted snugly into it. Her worries about Ross showed how much she valued her safe little world. In the aftermath of the storm, normality had its own sweet beauty.

She automatically began to wash up. It didn't take long. Making herself a cup of tea, she sat at the pine table, her chin propped in her hands as she tried to work out her feelings with regard to Ross's return. Instead her thoughts returned to the past.

The summer had been long and hot, she remembered. Even Saxonbridge, where the sea mists often brought gloom and chill, had felt the swelter of sunshine. Where better than England in the sunshine? The smell of fern, scorched grass, dusty heather, the placidity of gaily coloured caravans and tents etched by blue sky had combined to give that summer a dream quality. Saxonbridge had acquired a Mediterranean flavour; heat and colour abounded everywhere.

Scarlett had spent the summer in skimpy shorts and even skimpier T-shirts. Her hair just missed being red and she tanned if she was careful not to rush it. That summer, she had acquired a golden hue, her hair, eyes and skin merging into a picture of youthful beauty that had made many of the local youths and holiday-makers nudge each other and stare.

'God, I was so naïve—so brazen,' she muttered but her eyes held that preoccupied look, caught in memory.

She had gone with David to a disco with a crowd of their friends to celebrate his birthday. They'd had a family party at the farm but that night they had intended to have the informal version and spirits were high. They had all piled into the Land Rover. Unfortunately David had drunk far too much, an unusual occurrence for him, caused by the unsuccessful pursuit of a girl called Stephanie. When Scarlett had brought up the problem of getting home, he had said they'd sleep on the beach. Aware of the rumpus that would cause in the McQuillan camp, she had called the farm and Ross had listened to her explanation with bored patience.

'I suppose I'd better come and get you,' he said. 'I'd suggest a bed and breakfast but at seventeen economy might get in the way of discretion.'

She didn't realise until she had put the receiver down that she had been insulted. Ross clearly thought she would fall into bed with the nearest male purely as a matter of economic convenience. He was totally misled with regard to her morals but it said a lot about his own. She couldn't imagine him at seventeen, having to phone home to get picked up. She wished David had been more sensible; as it was she had to play nursemaid until the hateful Ross McQuillan turned up.

Ross arrived at one o'clock in the morning, by which time most of the crowd had dispersed and a few stragglers remained. He had brought the horsebox and unceremoniously dumped the worst casualities of the night's excesses into the back. David went with them and then Ross locked the back in case anyone had the bright idea of trying to get out while they were on the road. Scarlett had to travel in the front with him.

'Are the others OK?' He broke the ice after he had negotiated the van back on to the road.

'Yes. Some were camping.'

'It shows a degree of forethought,' he commended. 'Why did David get drunk? Did you give him the brush-off?'

Scarlett turned her head to look at him, frowning. 'No. He's not interested in me, it was——' She didn't continue, not wishing to reveal her friend's confidences.

'I didn't mean to pry.' He was darkly sarcastic. In fact everything about him was dark. He was dressed in full evening dress. His hair was black, his eyes a shade lighter and his jaw was darkened by stubble especially thick on his upper lip. 'If I were his age and you were haunting the house, I think I'd be interested.' A smile curled his mouth but he kept his eyes on the road and she was astonished at his ease with such a revelation. Scarlett felt hot and cold and her stomach was alive with butterflies. No one had ever said anything like that to her before.

'David's my friend.' She was defensive. 'It is possible, you know, even at seventeen, to have a friend of the opposite sex.'

His smile turned into a grin; he didn't say anything in response but surprisingly changed the subject.

'Have you heard from your parents recently?'

She was startled, suspecting his motives. 'I had a letter last month. They're inclined to be erratic. I expect the post isn't very reliable.'

'That must be it.' He looked irritated by something. 'Do you miss them?'

She shrugged negligently. 'They've got their own lives. I respect what they do. I'm old enough to look after myself.'

His derisive snort showed what he thought of that. 'Sleeping rough in Scarborough, with only a drunk for protection, isn't very smart. It's a bank holiday, bikers' paradise——'

'I called you,' she pointed out crossly. 'And I would have slept in the car. You're a fine one to preach about being careful; your mother never stops worrying about you.'

He laughed at that, his eyes narrowing as a car failed to dip its headlights coming in the opposite direction. 'In my game, you learn to follow certain rules. It doesn't always work but ninety per cent of the time it gets you through. Do you like living at Saxonbridge? Your mother might think you're responsible enough but I bet mine keeps you on a tight leash.'

Scarlett wrapped her arms around her body trying to conserve heat; she had been chilled by the long wait for Ross to arrive.

'I'm not a hooligan. I mix with the same crowd as David; she knows most of them. I'm perfectly aware of how to behave when I'm a guest in someone else's house.'

'Prickly little thing, aren't you?'

'And I expect you have an opinion on everything,' she returned, trying to stop her teeth from chattering.

'Most things,' he agreed, slowing down and bringing the van to a halt in a gravelled lay-by.

Scarlett tensed, as he shrugged out of his jacket. The engine growled like a big cat on a chain, the dim light from the dashboard carving his face in shadowed relief. She felt his body heat reach out to her and a spasm of shivering shook her, more to do with the sudden intimacy of the situation than the cold.

'Here.' He placed the warm jacket around her shoulders. 'The heater's broken.' His voice had a warm, rough texture to it, as if kindness was something he was uncomfortable with.

'Thank you.' A little stunned by his consideration, she watched him as he negotiated the horse van back on to the road. The jacket engulfed her, his scent pleasant in her nostrils, and Scarlett became keenly aware of the mysterious aura of sexual power surrounding this adult male. She felt a growing fascination, as he deposited the young men back at their homes, at his control over the situation. He exchanged a few humorous comments with their parents, an indulgent adult bringing back bad boys from a teenage rampage.

When they arrived back at the farm, he heaved David over his shoulder and carried him up to his bedroom, complaining about the smell left over from the horsebox.

John McQuillan appeared on the landing, looking down over the banister to see Scarlett still in possession of Ross's jacket and his elder son quietly in the process of shutting David's door.

'They're back, then.' His gruff Yorkshire accent sounded loud on the night air.

'Scarlett called.'

'Aye, well, it's time she was in bed too. Come on, young lady.' He beckoned her up the stairs. 'Joanne rang but I said you'd be late back and not to wait up.'

'Thanks, Dad.' Ross's tone was drily amused. He took the jacket as Scarlett passed him on the stairs and followed leisurely in her wake.

That had been the start of it. Scarlett swallowed thickly. She had never had any problem sharing the house with David but Ross's presence had changed everything that summer. She became highly sensitised to everything about him—everything that belonged to him. He would wander about the house in shorts when it was hot, his body brown and muscular. Scarlett would watch him surreptitiously, fascinated by his every movement. She had even offered to help with the ironing just to have the pleasure of smoothing the creases out of his shirts.

It would all have ended as a harmless crush, she decided, had it not been for a letter from her parents telling her that they would not be able to get away for the promised summer holiday. She had never needed the security and advice her parents could give more and they couldn't fit her in. It had suddenly hurt so much that the pain was unbearable.

Flinging the letter on to her bedroom floor, she had left the house in a fit of desperation. She had walked for miles and finally flung herself down in the shelter of a small, heather-clad hill and cried with all the passion and heartache of her tender years.

She must have slept because Ross had woken her, his hand gentle on her shoulder, his eyes warm and compassionate.

'What do you want?' She had scrubbed at her face with her hands, trying to disguise the tear-stains.

'To take you home. You can't stay out here all night, sweetheart; it's getting dark.'

'Why not? It's not as if anyone really cares, is it? I don't suppose it occurs to—Mum and Dad that their friends might get fed up with having a permanent house guest.'

'I expect when facing human tragedy social niceties don't count for much,' he reflected wryly.

'No.' Her voice was hollow. 'I suppose you think I'm selfish.'

'No.' His hand brushed her cheek gently. 'Sometimes things aren't right or wrong, but it doesn't stop them hurting.'

'Well, thank you for putting it in perspective.' She was mockingly polite. 'You can go now.'

'Bitch away, I've got a thick skin.' Leaning back against the gentle incline of the hill, he let his eyes wander to the brilliant gold and red of the dying sun. 'I'm not leaving you here, so cry it out and then we'll go back.'

'Stop treating me like a child,' she raged at him, leaning over him, her arm above his head to support her.

'Stop behaving like one, then!' His dark eyes surveyed her broodingly. 'Before very much longer, you're going to find a man who can take all the emotion you've got and want more. You'll leave childish things behind. You'll make time for your parents rather than them make time for you. Maybe they'll regret what they've lost but that's the way things are; there's no going back.'

'You speak as if you've lived all my emotions. You aren't me!' she protested fervently. 'You don't know how I feel!'

'I know something you don't.' He pulled the arm supporting her away and rolled her underneath him in one movement. 'Don't push me to prove it to you.'

Scarlett gazed up at him in shocked amazement. 'Ross——?'

'I'm getting out of the house tomorrow.' His dark eyes ran over her like a black wave. 'I can't keep taking cold showers.' He smiled but it didn't dilute the power of his gaze. 'I'm talking about sex, Scarlett; find someone to love you.'

'I don't want you to go!' The thought appalled her, and she ignored his warning. 'Please don't.' She wrapped her arms around his neck, her youthful ardency fuelled by the threat of his departure.

'Scarlett——'

Her mouth found his and clung, despite his attempt to break the kiss, her lips brushing his ear as he turned away, her breath rushing against the sensitive surface and making him shudder. She pushed up the vest T-shirt he wore, her hands roaming over his skin.

'Scarlett, this is crazy. I'm off to the Middle East——'

Shutting off the words she didn't want to hear was a compulsion and her mouth tempted his until she felt the pressure returned in a hard, male response that created shock-waves throughout her body.

'God, I must be crazy,' he muttered against her lips. 'I can't think straight when you're near me.'

The words failed to make an impression. Scarlett was burning with a fever that needed quenching, her golden beauty given with bounteous generosity on that heather-clad hillside bathed in crimson sunlight.

It was hard to accept that their relationship was something she couldn't acknowledge. Common sense told her that if anyone found out that Ross and she were lovers then she would have to leave the house. Ross was deep in his own thoughts on the way back to Saxonbridge, holding her hand until they got in sight of the house.

'Just go to your room. I'll tell them you need to rest. What happened out there is between you and me; the whole world doesn't have to know.' He mirrored her own thoughts but it still left her feeling disappointed.

'You won't leave tomorrow, will you?' she pleaded, her heart in her eyes.

'No. But you've got to understand, what happened today was a mistake. I'm not what you're looking for, Scarlett; I'd make you unhappy.'

Truer words had never been said! Scarlett blinked and returned to the cosy world of her kitchen, her dazed expression showing just how much she had become entwined with the past. She had pushed that other Scarlett to the back of her mind, forgetting how vulnerable she had been and how despicable of Ross to take advantage! He had clearly been aware of her fawning admiration and had been excited by it. It hadn't taken much for him to forget his scruples and take what she offered. It was even more reprehensible considering his on-off relationship with Joanne Williams.

The days before he left had been a torture of simmering passions barely controlled. Ross had been determined not to repeat his 'mistake' and had endeavoured to cool things between them. Scarlett had brooded with the intensity of youth and the atmosphere between them whenever they were alone had been electric. She had followed him into the barn, watching him as he stacked bales of hay for the coming winter. Clad in a pair of faded denims, naked from the waist up, his muscles moving under his tanned skin, he had been an object of fascination to Scarlett. He had caught her gaze, turning his head swiftly as if he sensed her presence.

Taking up his T-shirt, he had used it to wipe around his neck, his eyes black in the dim light.

'You're making this hard, Scarlett,' he grated, a muscle tightening in his jaw. 'If I gave in to my baser instincts I'd take what you're offering. All that's stopping me is the knowledge that I'd make more of a mess of things than I've done already.'

'I love you,' Scarlett declared fervently. 'How can that be wrong?'

'You weren't sobbing your heart out on that hill for me, were you?' he pointed out grimly. 'It was a harmless crush until then. You were upset. Your parents let you down once too often and I made it worse by offering the wrong sort of comfort.' Sighing, he put the T-shirt back on and came a little closer. 'When I come home from the Middle East we'll talk about it again. You'll be eighteen soon; that sounds a little more respectable.' His gaze softened at her brightening expression. 'That's if I'm not yesterday's news by then.'

'You won't be,' she promised, rushing into his arms, to have him hold her comfortingly but without passion.

'My father knows how to get in touch with me if you need me.' His breath feathered her hair and she looked up at him uncomprehendingly.

'We weren't exactly careful out there on the moor,' he reminded her gently. 'It's fairly unlikely that there will be repercussions but——'

Scarlett blushed bright red at the very thought. Ross kissed her forehead and urged her out of the barn. It was the last time she was alone with him before he went to the Middle East.

It took all her strength not to make a scene when he left. She tried to pretend that her mature attitude would make him realise she was ready for a serious relationship. She fooled herself into believing her youth was the only thing stopping them being together.

Every day she awaited the postman hopefully but nothing came. Ross sent postcards to all the family, none to her in particular. She watched every news broadcast, scared stiff he would be killed or taken hostage by some shadowy terrorist group. He repaid her devotion by taking himself off on holiday to the Bahamas instead of coming home. She was miserable and had started feeling the symptoms of her pregnancy. Mary McQuillan shrewdly guessed what was wrong with her and in an emotional confrontation the whole thing came out into the open. Ross was summoned, returned to face the music and fell in with the hastily made wedding plans. Their marriage, nine months in duration, had moments of tenderness, times when Scarlett briefly rode the crest of the wave merely to crash down again into the depths of despair when he left her and put his life on the line for another woman.

Scarlett's eyes hardened at the memory. Let the McQuillans welcome home the prodigal son, but she hadn't forgotten how it felt to be left alone to cope with a young baby. She didn't wish him back to oblivion, she hadn't it in her to be vindictive, but she did hope he would continue his gypsy lifestyle and prove a minor disturbance in her otherwise peaceful existence.

CHAPTER TWO

THE McQuillan's home was a large, picturesque house, clad in sandstone, the mellow golden walls dusted by the rough edge of time to give a graceful effect of strength and beauty that melded perfectly with the character of the area. Two red setters scampered up to Scarlett as she approached the house from the private road, the entrance to which was marked by the gatehouse. Drake and Karis were show dogs but although well groomed were allowed the freedom their exuberance demanded. They knew better than to chase the sheep that dotted McQuillan land wherever you looked. Absently fielding their advances, Scarlett saw the door opening ahead of her. For once, she guessed, she had suddenly become more than a pawn in the McQuillan dynasty. Squaring her shoulders, she greeted her mother-in-law, who smiled but couldn't dim the wariness that marked her expression.

'Come in, Scarlett. Have you eaten? I don't think any of us has had regular meals since Ross returned. Did you see him on the news? We've been hounded by the Press since I told Leila Holbrook.'

Leila Holbrook was Mary's best friend whose son worked on the *Gazette*. It was inevitable that Ross's return would cause a stir. He was a celebrity.

'No, I was too busy getting Jordan off to school. Is Ross in? I wanted to talk to him before he meets Jordan.'

'He's on the phone to Rio de Janeiro. He has things to tie up there apparently.'

Probably explaining his acquisition of a family to some South American beauty, Scarlett thought bitchily.

The lounge hadn't changed that much in the six years Ross had been away. Mary McQuillan hadn't the heart for redecoration and the paintwork had merely been freshened up, the faded pale blue velvet chairs and couch comfortable without being shabby. The room was south-facing and therefore abundant in light, drawing in the April sunshine, the pale beige carpet and cream walls combining with stripped-pine floors and shelving in the alcoves packed with books.

Scarlett was surprised to find the family assembled; even Jeanette, David's wife, was there. She glanced around the room with a sudden foreboding which didn't take long to be comfirmed.

'Scarlett,' John McQuillan began in a gruff embarrassed tone. 'We wanted a word before you see Ross.'

'What about?' A familiar feeling of being manipulated into doing 'what was right' came over her. 'I'm perfectly prepared to discuss Jordan in a reasonable manner. I won't dwell on the past if that's causing concern.'

Mary McQuillan looked as if she was about to burst into indignant speech but David forestalled her.

'Don't be so defensive, Scarlett. Nobody expects you to resume your marriage with Ross as if nothing had happened. But your attitude towards him is as if you've been separated rather than parted by circumstances. It's going to be hard, you realise that; being presented with a divorce petition on his arrival is hardly a gentle introduction to family life.'

Scarlett swallowed thickly. 'I have my own life, David. Philip is hardly going to understand——'

'Philip!' Mary McQuillan was scathing. 'It comes to something when a doctor should associate with a married woman. If you had any sense you'd get rid of him before Ross discovers the whole sordid affair.'

Scarlett's spine stiffened, her eyes glinting. 'It is not an affair. Philip and I are friends.' Her experience with Ross had been a salutary lesson. 'I no longer rush into anything before thinking first.'

'You don't love Philip, Scarlett,' Jeanette appealed to her with sympathy in her eyes. 'Love isn't planned——'

'Love' hardly graced what Scarlett remembered of Ross. He certainly hadn't loved her and she had been too young to know the difference between love and infatuation. She sighed, not liking the fact that she was upsetting everyone but unable to come to terms with their expectations. Ross wouldn't want to get involved with her again! Time would resolve the dilemma; there was no reason to antagonise the family.

'I think the best thing for me to do is to talk to Ross alone. I won't act hastily but I'm not making any promises as to the result.' It occurred to her that she had grown up; indeed, hadn't Ross said much the same thing to her after they'd made love on the moor? 'No promises' summed up their relationship. He'd be proud of her maturity, she thought cynically, although she still couldn't measure up to him when it came to self-interest.

As if summoned by her thoughts, Ross paused in the doorway, leaning against the door-jamb and regarding the gathering of the clan.

'Scarlett,' he greeted her. 'Where's the boy?'

'Jordan's at school. I thought you could meet him this evening. We need to talk first.' Her eyes told him how much she resented what had been going on in the room and he picked up on the undertone of tension with ease.

'OK.' Smiling at his new-found family, he was none the less determined that the discussion should not be for public airing. 'Excuse us. Scarlett?' He beckoned her to join him and she followed him, surprised when he collected his jacket and led the way out of the house.

'Where are we going?' she asked, frowning.

'Somewhere else.' He flicked her a derisive look over his shoulder. 'Somewhere you can shout.'

She was unnerved by his accuracy in reading her frustration. She blinked with surprise as she saw the car; it was a Rolls, a Silver Shadow. It looked singularly out of place in the courtyard of Saxonbridge Farm.

'What makes you think I want to shout?' she enquired coolly, settling into the luxurious depths of the car seat with reluctant appreciation.

'Your eyes. You've been accusing me of something since the moment we met—sorry, since we re-met.'

'I——'

He ignored her fledgeling attempt to deny his words, casting her a knowing glance before firing the engine of the magnificent machine, effectively cutting off whatever it was she was trying to say.

It was the oddest feeling. Ross was immediate in a way that shocked her. He didn't pussyfoot about being polite, he was straight in there, challenging her less-than-warm reception.

'I get the impression you're not too thrilled about my return.' Ross flicked her a glance of sardonic amusement. 'Would you have preferred me to remain dead?'

'No!' She was aghast at the thought. 'I never wished you dead, Ross.' Boiled slowly in oil, maybe, but not dead.

He accepted this, turning the car on to the road heading towards Robin Hood's Bay. 'Was I turned on by all that starchy respectability or are you a reformed teenage wildcat?'

His description made her eyes ignite and he laughed, enjoying the conflagration.

'I don't think there's much point in dwelling on the past.' She tried to be cool and reasonable and sounded resentful.

'We have joint responsibilities. Besides, I'd like to know what I'm accused of. I presume I got you pregnant. Even if I was knocked out by that red-gold hair and those tiger eyes, I don't think I'd have planned a family so quickly.'

Scarlett felt her fingernails dig into the upholstery, seeking the familiar countryside which swept down towards the cliff-face, avoiding the challenge of his eyes.

'Well?' He demanded an answer and Scarlett gave him one through stiff lips.

'The usual story of a young girl besotted with an older man. Now you know, perhaps we can leave the issue.'

'We're still married,' he pointed out. 'That's going to take some thinking about.'

Scarlett failed to reply, the McQuillans' pleas ringing in her ears.

'Is there another man involved? You're young and attractive, despite your attempt to dim your appeal with shapeless clothes.'

'I have a friend, yes. But it's no more than that, despite what your mother may think.'

'Mother-in-law syndrome, huh? I thought so.'

'Well, aren't you the bright one.' Scarlett's decision to be reasonable and discuss Jordan seemed to have been subverted. It was the gibe about her clothes that had got under her skin. How dared he come back after six years and tell her she was dowdy?

'So you've been celibate all this time?' He whistled with admiration. 'Didn't you like sex?'

'I beg your pardon?'

'Didn't——?'

'I heard what you said. I was merely expressing disbelief that you feel this sort of conversation is necessary. I can quite believe you've mown your way through the beauties of Brazil but I got my fingers burnt on your dubious attractions and I don't intend to be deluded that sex is equated with anything worthwhile in terms of stability.'

'Stability.' He tested the word as if it was foreign to him. 'Pipe and slippers by the hearth, you mean? This friend, does he fit the picture?'

'Yes, he does actually. He's a doctor and he's very caring.'

'But a bit of a disappointment with regard to the bedside manner?'

'We were supposed to be discussing Jordan,' she reminded him frigidly.

'OK.' He turned the car off the main road and parked, a vista of sheep-nibbled green fields and dry stone walls providing all the space and privacy they needed. Apart from some distant ramblers, walking part of the Cleveland Way, there was no one in shouting distance. Getting out, he gestured her to follow with a smart tattoo on the bonnet and walked off towards the cliff, with her reluctantly in his wake.

Looking daggers at his back, she summed up the picture of swaggering masculinity with grudging attention to detail. His jacket was new, the still strong smell of leather lingering in her nostrils. It was chocolate-brown with a suede trim and his jeans were well worn and fitted him like a glove. A claret-coloured sweater defended him from the sharp spring breeze, his black hair spiking the collar of the denim shirt he wore underneath.

Once his machismo had appealed to her. She had liked the way other women's eyes were drawn to him and had possessively linked his arm, queening it over them. Youth, she reflected, was curiously blinkered. Possessing a man attractive to any female with active hormones was a curse, not a blessing, and she had soon learnt her lesson.

'OK. You have my undivided attention.' Ross perched on a flat piece of wall, inviting her to sit beside him but she refused, preferring not to be within touching distance. Acknowledging the fact, his eyes glittered dangerously.

'So scared,' he murmured and she glared back at him.

'Your business in Brazil.' She determinedly brought the subject around to his future. 'Presumably you've built a life for yourself there. Six years is a long time. Do you have ties there, someone to return to?'

He watched her chin tilt up and read what even she didn't perceive about her own system of defence.

'No. I've got friends. There have been women passing through my hotels who wanted something casual and that suited me. Nothing permanent.'

'Sounds wonderful.'

'I'm careful; I have no other children and a clean bill of health. Anything else you want to know?'

'I don't want to know anything,' she spat. 'I'm merely assessing how likely it is that you'll be around long enough to belatedly fill your role as Jordan's father.'

'Curious and curiouser,' he murmured with soft provocation. 'What have I done?'

'Nothing you wouldn't do again, I'm sure.'

'Undoubtedly,' he agreed, his eyes wandering from her breasts to her lips with undisguised appreciation.

'Jordan!' she stipulated desperately.

Smiling slowly, he enjoyed her lack of composure. 'I've thought about it. I like the kid; he's got guts. Being a father appeals to me and something about this feels right.' He gestured expansively to the enduring landscape.

Scarlett's heart sank. He was going to stay! She had hoped he would have found his new life too exotic to leave permanently.

'Sorry to disappoint you, tiger, but I'm not going anywhere. How do you want me to play it with Jordan? Shall I come over to the gatehouse or will you bring him to the farm?'

'Come to the house for tea,' she offered without enthusiasm.

Later, she mulled over the conversation. He had deliberately provoked her, she realised with a belated rush of comprehension. Ross wouldn't be happy until he had the whole unhappy episode of their marriage out in the open and thoroughly dissected. It disturbed her that he still had the power to make her feel vulnerable. Not vulnerable in the old way, where he could bruise her with a look, but creating that unwelcome feeling that things weren't quite as controlled as she liked to think.

Philip Parker called in at the gatehouse late that afternoon. He often popped in if he had a slack patch and he saw evidence of activity.

Philip was a nice man, his fair hair curling close to his head, blue eyes considerate and understanding. He had seen the news about Ross McQuillan on the TV and was eager to discuss it with her.

'Mary was right, then,' he reflected. 'Mother's intuition, I suppose. It must have been a shock for you, pet; how are you bearing up?'

'Still reeling.' She eyed him curiously. Sometimes, she did feel she was getting a consultation rather than a personal conversation but she supposed it was just his manner. 'Speculation must be high. I mean, Ross and I have no future together but——'

'Mmm, I've had some veiled comments already. We'll have to keep to form for a while until you've sorted something out. Being a GP is a mixed blessing. All the old biddies will be watching us like hawks.'

Scarlett accepted this, although she couldn't remember a time they hadn't kept to form. It was nice of him to be so understanding. She didn't want unjust gossip tainting their relationship; she had Jordan to think about. The farming community was small and tight-knit; everybody knew each other's business. Ross coming back and her friendship with the unattached GP would keep bored tongues wagging for weeks.

Philip's paging machine bleeped and he pulled a face, taking a hasty swallow of tea. 'Can I use the phone?' he requested, on his way into the passage.

Scarlett answer was purely rhetorical as he was already using it. She saw him to the door, received a brief peck on the cheek and was beset with a sudden deep frustration that was distinctly upsetting. She suddenly recalled what Ross had once said to her.

'I'm talking about sex, Scarlett; find someone to love you.' Had she done that? Did Philip love her or was she just running away from the ferocity of her youthful passion?

Jordan's interest in his father had been fuelled by the talk of his schoolfriends. Scarlett felt the speculation on the air when she collected her son from his school in Whitby. Fielding congratulations on her supposed good luck, she returned to the gatehouse to find several reporters camped outside in a Volvo.

'Why are those men there, Mum?' Jordan peered through the window. 'Shall I get Grandad to bring the dogs?'

'No.' Scarlett was appalled by the bloodthirsty instincts of her child. 'They'll soon get bored. They're interested in your daddy. They're from the newspapers.'

'Oh.' Jordan was even more curious and keeping him away from the windows was impossible.

'Wow!' he exclaimed, when she was peering into the oven at the steak pie she had made. 'What a car! Come and see this, Mum.'

Realising her son would be intrigued by Ross's choice in transport, she reluctantly joined him.

'That's—er—your father.'

Jordan went quiet, watching the reporters desert their car and come running up. Ross fielded them off easily and pushed his way into the house.

'The news must be boring.' He jerked his dark head to the door. 'I've got reporters coming out of the woodwork.'

'So have we,' she returned sweetly. Then, realising she couldn't continue where she had left off that morning in front of Jordan, she smiled in welcome.

'Jordan.' She glanced behind her to see her son peeping past her. What did she say? It sounded odd introducing Jordan to Ross.

'We met last night.' Ross took over. 'He was looking after you. He wouldn't let me in.'

'I didn't know you were my dad.' Jordan was indignant.

'You did the right thing. I could have been anyone.' He pulled a package out from inside his jacket. 'Your grandmother tells me you like cars. I thought you might like this.' He gave Jordan a thick glossy book with a series of cards to stick in appropriate places.

'Terrific!' Jordan was enthused, his eyes shining. 'Can I have a ride in your car?'

'Of course.' Ross smiled. 'When those reporters have gone away.'

Scarlett endured the ease with which Ross included himself in sorting out the cards and searching through the book to find the appropriate places to stick them in. Children were sponges as far as attention was concerned and a knowledgeable male willing to talk cars was Jordan's idea of paradise.

Ross shared their evening meal, offered to wash up afterwards, and Jordan clumsily helped as they gave Scarlett 'a rest'. Gales of laughter came from the kitchen and she scowled at the separating door.

When Jordan had gone to bed, a protracted process in itself, she returned from letting her son know that his pocket money was forfeit if he came down one more time, to find Ross had made her a cup of coffee.

'Coffee for the demon mother.' He grinned at her flushed cheeks. 'You made my ears ring.'

'Children don't take you seriously at anything under ninety decibels,' she retorted with a glint in her eyes. 'I hope you're a car enthusiast; if you're just pretending Jordan will hound you to death.'

'It's one of my passions,' he confirmed, a lurking appreciation in his eyes, unsubtly hinting at more adult interests.

Scarlett had donned fashionable leggings and top which made her look young and healthy, the striped top matched by the beige leggings suiting her colouring.

'When did you turn into a mum? I have some very erotic dreams about a gorgeous redhead with tiger's eyes.'

'You're making it up!' she accused, not willing to be any part of his dreams, erotic or otherwise.

'I thought so,' he agreed, his eyes running over her with blatant male curiosity. 'But if you've got a small mole the shape of a teardrop inside your right shoulder-blade then——' He laughed as she went bright red. 'Honey, if that's true, there's a lot you're keeping repressed and it can't be healthy.'

'Don't call me honey! And keep all your seduction stuff for those gullible enough to fall for it.'

His eyes smiled into hers. 'You almost believe this act, don't you? Did the shock of the crash do this to you or did I?'

Mutinously, she regarded him, her topaz eyes telling him she wouldn't be drawn and there was nothing she'd like more than to slap his face.

'My mother's giving a party tomorrow night. There'll be other children there for Jordan; I'd like you to come.'

'Very well.' She knew it would cause gossip if she followed her instincts and refused to go and Jordan wouldn't think much of being left out of a party.

'I'm giving a Press conference; that should get rid of the monkeys outside. Don't let them bother you. If they do anything intrusive, call the farm.'

'I can handle reporters, should they intrude.' She gave him a speaking look and he pressed his lips together, subduing a smile.

'Goodnight.' He went to the door. 'He's a great kid.'

'A kid is a baby goat.'

'Sorry, Mum.' He smirked. 'If you come to me tonight, I'll send you back to your unsullied bed.'

'Just go, please.' Her patience was shredding fast. It was with utmost relief that she saw the door close behind his infuriating figure and she collapsed into a chair feeling utterly drained.

Scarlett went to work as usual on the Friday morning. Jordan went reluctantly to school, not appreciating her insistence on normality; he wanted to go up to the farm.

She had not taken much from Ross's bank but she had used some of the money to open a tea-shop in Whitby. It was early in the season for the main bustle of holiday trade but Whitby's tourism had grown with the popularity of various TV programmes that showed the beauty of the Dales as a backcloth to their main content. It was also a stopping-off point for ramblers walking the Cleveland Way and drew from nearby industrial towns, when their inhabitants wanted some fresh sea air regardless of the season.

She couldn't park near the café and usually left her car up by the abbey. A series of shallow steps brought her down from the cliff walk into the town. There were reputedly one hundred and ninety-nine. Jordan repeatedly counted them but Scarlett was willing to believe the tourist blurb.

The wind whipped her hair back from her face, her eyes taking in the mouth of the River Esk as it met the sea, the arms of the harbour providing a safe haven for ships and boats alike. It was an old town, built higgledy-piggledy near the river, the red roofs of Whitby town making her heart swell with a familiar feeling of love. Above her, the seagulls called urgently, swinging through the air over the river and on to where the seaside take-aways provided a good source of food.

Her own café, Ramblers, did a mixture of traditional fish and chips with popular additions like chilli con carne and jacket potatoes with various fillings. The kitchens were set back from the serving area and allowed for none of the noise and clatter of food preparation that marked some of her rivals.

Tracy Hope, a local girl who worked for her, was already making the morning cup of tea when she got in. Tracy sometimes looked after Jordan and was a pleasant girl, with an irrepressible sense of humour. She had a round face, with dark hair and big blue eyes.

'I didn't think you'd be in. The *Gazette* rang but I said you were staying at the house.'

'Thanks. I'll keep a low profile in the kitchen. I suppose it will be over in a few days.'

'The papers will be after his story. Ross will be able to write it himself, won't he? They're bound to want a picture of you. How do you fancy being on the front page of the dailies?'

'Don't!' she pleaded with deep abhorrence. It was bad enough having her local community absorbed in Ross's return without the whole nation focusing in on it. It was to be expected, she supposed; he had been an international reporter as well as a best-selling author, and with such a spectacular story behind him he was going to be the focus of a lot of attention.

'I'd like to be famous,' Tracy reflected. 'I know you don't like publicity much but don't let that fraud Joanne Williams knock you out of the limelight. She was gushing like a tap last night on TV; did you see her?'

'No.' Scarlett tensed as another skeleton stepped out of the cupboard. Joanne Williams! She remembered, all too well, the interview when the woman was asked why she didn't board the helicopter with Ross. The woman had hinted at her hero having unfinished business at home. The wistful pain in Joanne Williams's eyes hadn't suggested that Ross had been rushing back into the arms of his family. Scarlett hadn't had to rack her brains too hard to imagine the confrontation she would have had with Ross if the plane hadn't crashed.

Mary McQuillan would have adored Joanne as a daughter-in-law. Mr and Mrs Glitz would have made her the envy of the Dales; instead she had been lumbered with an immature seventeen-year-old who refused to be moulded.

'It's bound to be strange at first. People don't change, though, do they? Not deep down.' Tracy clearly thought Scarlett was startled by that comment, her own opinions the reverse. She had changed, thank God. There was nothing left of that naïve teenager impressed by the power of an older man.

'I think you'll find bringing up a child alone on my part and being lost in Brazil on Ross's changes everything. We're strangers, Tracy; you can forget any ideas of a romantic reunion.'

It was an unusually busy day in the café, which made Scarlett reflect on her sudden notoriety. Tracy had revealed that many of the customers commented on Ross's return. She had momentarily gone through to the café to help Tracy at the till and ten minutes later the Press had arrived, proving that the café had been under surveillance. She had refused to answer any questions and returned to the gatehouse that night to find several reporters at her door. It seemed inevitable that certain aspects of her personal life were about to become public knowledge.

Keeping her temper, she busied herself getting Jordan bathed and putting out his clothes for the 'party' that night. She wished she could share in his excitement. She felt as if she had an appointment with the guillotine.

'Will Daddy have brought me sweets and presents?' Jordan asked as his hair was dried and brushed into order.

'Daddy isn't Santa Claus. It's just good that he's home. You're not to ask for anything. Grandma will have nice things for you; I don't think you'll come back empty-handed.'

'I hope there's jelly with strawberries in it,' he said, round-eyed.

'Grandma knows you like it; I expect there will be jelly.'

She left him to get dressed with strict instructions to 'keep clean'. She might have mixed feelings about Ross but she didn't want him to think he'd fathered a ragamuffin.

For her own part, she was in a quandary what to wear. She had several suitable dresses in the wardrobe that were smart but for some reason none of them appealed. She had nothing exotic and she realised that most of her clothes were pedestrian in nature. Deciding, finally, on a black two-piece enlivened by a flower design in mauve and primrose, she added a gold watch and small pearl earrings. Her hair she wore swept back from her forehead, the red-gold waves falling to her shoulders. As she stood at her mirror her topaz eyes returned her interest, trouble in their depths.

She heard the soft swish of tyres outside and looked out, her eyes widening as she saw Ross get out of the vehicle. He suited formal clothes, she was reluctantly forced to admit.

Jordan ran to the door and Scarlett followed him, her heart beating hard against her ribs. It was stupid to feel so nervous but she couldn't help it. The physical presence of the man was hard to ignore. The power she had sensed in him hadn't been an adolescent fantasy, it was still there, stronger than ever. His comments on her appearance made her feel she had made an effort just for him, which wasn't true! Everyone liked to look nice for a party.

'Get in the car,' he instructed, his dark eyes flashing to the photographer who was determined to get a family picture.

Scarlett obeyed, sitting in the back with Jordan, who had to be physically restrained from hanging over the driver's seat to ogle the dashboard.

'What a wonderful piece of machinery,' he breathed in a voice that was reminiscent of Ross's comments the evening before. She saw Ross smile as he slid into the driver's seat, no doubt flattered that his son should mimic him.

'The interview I did with Yorkshire TV should go out tonight. Interest should wane after that. I suppose a young, beautiful wife and the acquisition of Jordan might keep us high-profile for a while. It's the kind of sentimental slush that sells newspapers.'

'I think you might find it a little more complicated than that.' Scarlett was sweetness and light. 'Your old friend Joanne Williams doesn't share my dislike of public exposure and she's sure to want to thank you for all you did for her.'

'Joanne?'

'She will be disappointed if you've forgotten her.' Acid dripped from her tongue. 'But no doubt perfectly willing to catch up on old times.'

'There's only one woman in my dreams, baby, and we've already established that's you.' He smiled at her in the rear-view mirror and she gave an irritated 'tut', wishing a small corner in her heart didn't soften at his words. 'We're both older and wiser, Scarlett; it would help if you would stop sulking about the past and get on with the future.'

'I'd be delighted to,' she responded with bitter humour. 'But the past has a habit of coming back.'

'My mum doesn't sulk, she's grown-up,' Jordan chirped in, reminding them that little pitchers had big ears and that they should be more discreet.

'No, of course not, I'm sorry.' Ross kept his voice level. 'Your mum's perfect; I'm sure she wouldn't disagree with that.'

Scarlett smiled at Jordan and he seemed to take this as evidence that things were all right.

Saxonbridge Farm was lit up like a Christmas tree. It was years since the courtyard had been crammed with expensive cars; Mary McQuillan was making up for lost time. Jordan scrambled out of the car, eager to investigate. Ross unwound himself from the driver's seat and came to open Scarlett's door for her. She beat him by seconds and then had to endure his eyes on her legs as she tried to disembark with as much grace as she could.

Catching her wrist, he stopped her before she could move off towards the house. 'I'd appreciate it if you didn't spend the evening avoiding me; you're the only one I know.'

'You have the rest of your family,' she pointed out, not wanting to feel any sympathy for his position. Mary McQuillan was eager to introduce her son to his past, as if by doing so she could convince herself that he was here in the present. It had to be a strain for Ross.

'Forget I asked.' His eyes were black with temper. 'After you——' He gestured with laboured politeness towards the house.

Scarlett sighed and fell in at his side. If Ross had been like David or Philip it would have been easy to support him while he was vulnerable, easy to be friends. But Ross was a different kind of animal, one that could purr and then savage without conscience.

Her memory, which had so far busily supplied her with images of pain and betrayal, confused her with a contrasting picture. She had a sudden vivid flash of the loving pride displayed on Ross's handsome features the first time he had held Jordan in his arms. The McQuillans had a strong sense of family; it was something that she admired in them. Scarlett decided that it wouldn't hurt her to extend a modicum of support to Ross that evening, even though she was sure he would manage admirably without it.

They entered the noisy hubbub together, Scarlett self-consciously tucking her hand into the crook of his arm. He had asked for her help and she would give it but he had to promise to behave in recognition of her support. Her eyes said as much when he glanced down at her in surprise.

Jordan came and took her free hand and Scarlett was overpoweringly conscious of the fact that she had made a tactical mistake. Sandwiched between her husband and her son, she had unwittingly been drawn into creating an image of a family that had a future before it. The shining eyes and warm smiles around her conveyed approval. She had made a dreadful mistake! And she had fallen into a trap...

CHAPTER THREE

ROSS stood by the hearth holding court. The glimpse of vulnerability Scarlett had witnessed earlier was now hard to imagine. He wore a charcoal double-breasted suit, his shirt white as snow, a crimson and gold tie clipped with a gold tie-pin. He was a tall man, several inches over six feet, his black hair gleaming in the firelight.

Scarlett stood beside him, beginning to understand how wearisome it was to have to tell the same story over and over again. The fascination with his memory loss was equally apparent. He was less forthcoming about this and Scarlett gathered it was a delicate subject.

'How did you find us?' Her own curiosity was pricked. 'You were asking for Saxonbridge Farm; did you remember the name?'

'To begin with I remembered the name Saxonbridge—not that it was a farm but I remembered the sea. For a while I thought I was an American. It wasn't until I met some English tourists in a bar who picked up the accent that I realised I was in fact English. I guess over the years I developed a transatlantic twang.'

'Didn't they recognise you?'

'They said I reminded them of somebody but that was a while after the crash. Reporters are soon forgotten.' He shrugged ironically.

'You eased off TV work to write,' she commented. He'd done that while she was pregnant, part of the false security she had been lulled into. It had been destroyed every time his friends had visited or they'd gone to a party with his old media colleagues and she'd had to watch him seduced back into the glittering world of show business.

'What took you so long to find us?'

'Money. Passport. In Brazil you're no one without cash. Saxonbridge was just a name; it didn't start to have real significance until this last year. I began to feel—remember just brief flashes of a past that was just out of reach. It haunted me.'

'Why didn't you try the embassy? They would have helped.'

'I did later. By that time, I guess the crash was history. Chad Mathews wasn't the type to contact officialdom and at the beginning I was stuck with his dubious reputation. When I discovered that wasn't my name, I was running a small bar in Marabá.'

'You thought you were on the run?'

A white grin slashed his dark features. 'That guy wasn't exactly popular. I picked up a few fights on his reputation; it didn't take me long to learn his history. There wasn't much to recommend him.'

'How terrible.' It must have been a nightmare waking up without a past and taking on a criminal's identity.

'Brazilian prisons don't have much going for them. I kept a low profile. By the time I did contact the embassy they thought I was a no-good trying to get a free ticket home.'

'Didn't you tell them about the crash?'

'I blanked that out. All I remember was waking up on the edge of a village. I was confused and my feet were in a bad state; I must have walked for miles. I can't remember. The Indians gave me refuge. When they found out who I was supposed to be they gave me food and water and an invitation to leave. I had to wait until I had the time and money to start searching.'

'Did it matter so much?'

His face stilled and he considered the whisky in his glass. 'That's cruel, Scarlett.'

'I meant to you. You didn't have much to go on.' A flush crept up her cheeks as she realised how awful that sounded.

Dark eyes assailed hers. 'Without the past, the future can easily be knocked apart. Had I married, I would have been a bigamist. I had to know and——' he let his eyes flicker to her lips '—there was something else I was looking for that I couldn't find.'

The fire seemed to lick from the hearth around her ankles and shoot flames screaming through her body. Scarlett didn't quite know what to do. She had never in her wildest dreams expected Ross to want her back! She had adjusted to his loss, convinced herself she had got over it. But the past had nothing to do with this, or at least very little. Ross wanted her! Quite blatantly, he was stripping her with his eyes and didn't attempt to hide it when the awareness of the fact marked her features. She was no longer a seventeen-year-old, susceptible to his teasing, and he wasn't treating her like one. She was an adult woman tangling with the man she had every reason to distrust, and she would be throwing away the wisdom of experience if she gave an inch of ground to Ross McQuillan.

'I wanted a word about that.' She moved away from the hearth, surprised to find her temperature didn't drop. Those lazy dark eyes followed her.

'Any time you like. But somewhere more private.'

'Now. And we don't need to be private. For my part in your rehabilitation, I want you to keep your nocturnal fantasies to yourself.'

'You know something?' He feathered her chin with his thumb, his jaw tensing as she pulled away. 'I think I'm rehabilitating you.'

'I don't think so.'

'It's the first time I've seen your legs.'

'I didn't dress for you, you conceited oaf!'

'No,' he agreed. 'That's not how I want you, but it's an improvement.'

Speechless, she glared at him in disbelief. Mary McQuillan came into view all smiles; she was having a lovely time and they both relented on the grudge match and tried to look sociable.

'I've videoed the evening news. You haven't seen the item they did on Ross, have you, Scarlett?'

'I don't think——' Ross looked distinctly uncomfortable.

'Didn't they get your best side?' Scarlett was insouciant.

She followed Mary McQuillan, glad of an excuse to escape his hateful presence. Before the interview there was a re-run showing footage of the remains of the crash and, inevitably, of Joanne Williams's very public vigil.

'Such a nice girl,' Mary twittered. 'We must invite her over.'

Scarlett bit back a remark about Joanne arriving whether they invited her or not. Then she tensed as Ross came on to the screen with a female interviewer, Penny Marsh, who was all teeth and smiles.

The interview covered much of the ground she was familiar with and then went on to expand on the early days of survival when Ross had stumbled out of the jungle and found work at the Serra Pelada goldmine. Drifters came and went, he revealed, no one asked questions, a man's past was his own. Ross reflected that in this environment, with victims of malaria, alcoholic poisoning and violent fights, his lack of memory was in no way remarkable. He was just another hobo down on his luck.

Speculating that a gold strike must have been how Ross managed to start up in business, Scarlett was jerked into awareness when Penny Marsh asked Ross about his family and the difficulties of fitting back into his old lifestyle.

'Time will tell.' The screen image oozed charm and sex appeal and the female interviewer was glowing. 'My wife and I have the right chemistry; whether we can share the same bathroom remains to be seen.'

'And Joanne?'

'I'll thank Joanne when I meet her. I expect she's a busy woman, so I can't say when that will be.' His smile was knowing and closed that avenue of enquiry quite firmly.

Scarlett bit her lip, glad that Mary had chosen only a selected few to witness her son's media performance.

Chemistry! How dared he tell the world that? It sounded as if they were attracted to each other. The only chemistry between them was his tendency to provoke her explosive temper.

Jeanette McQuillan pressed a glass of sherry into her hand. 'You look pale, Scarlett. Do you want to sit down?'

'No, thank you.'

Her sister-in-law squeezed her arm. 'If Joanne does come, at least she knows the score, hmm?'

Scarlett frowned uncomprehendingly. Was it possible that she wasn't the only one actually to disapprove of Joanne Williams's annexation of Ross's memory as if only she had a right to it? She had thought she was alone in that sensitivity.

Scarlett returned to the lounge; escaping Ross and then his TV image left her with a similar feeling of relief. David and Jeanette's son Barry had been given a junior computer game to celebrate Ross's return and Jordan was equally pleased with his Lego castle. Mary McQuillan had either bought the toys or guided him in their purchase.

'Scarlett.' Mary took her arm, drawing her into the family circle. David was releasing the cork from a bottle of champagne and the ensuing explosion made Jordan and his cousin laugh loudly while the frothy golden liquid was poured into crystal glasses.

Mary gave the children tumblers of lemonade so that they could join in and John McQuillan made the toast. Ross had managed to gravitate to Scarlett's side without her noticing. She had been showing Jordan the bubbles fizzing in her glass.

'Ross.' His father lifted his glass in a toast. 'Welcome home. I'd like to hope you'll stay put for a while, but if you can't, to safe returns.'

'Safe returns,' the family echoed the toast, Scarlett mouthing the sentiment with very mixed feelings.

'I'm not going anywhere.' His voice was very near to her ear. She turned instinctively and his lips brushed hers briefly, his gaze dark and seductive.

There was a moment of stunned silence until Jordan broke into the frozen circle asking his new-found father to help him with the castle. Ross moved away, happy to comply, and Scarlett found she could breathe again, resisting the temptation to touch her madly tingling lips.

Jeanette made her way to her sister-in-law's side, her eyes widening expressively. 'Phew!'

'Six years in Brazil must have been very boring.' Scarlett tried to pretend a light-heartedness she didn't feel. Jeanette smiled but her eyes were speculative.

Sipping her champagne, Scarlett rather spitefully hoped he would be a dead loss at Lego but again she was frustrated. He sat on the carpet with the boys, letting them make a mess of his carefully constructed castle and repairing it when they were absorbed elsewhere.

It was a happy family scene. Anyone peeping through the leaded windows would have seen three generations of McQuillans in supposed harmony. Mary McQuillan couldn't have been happier, her lace hanky fluttering to her eyes on several occasions. Knowing what it was to be a mother, Scarlett knew how much that day must have meant to her mother-in-law.

Surprisingly enough, it was John McQuillan who made the expected family appeal, and with not quite the approach she expected.

She was washing the dishes when her father-in-law came in and picked up a tea-towel.

The kitchen faced north and in the distance she could see the sea. Night was darkening the sky and the sheep moved in a desultory fashion across the carpet of green, lambs following the ewes in little scatters and rushes. She loved the land in all its moods, loved the harsh climate that could gentle in spring and burn in summer. She had been rootless until she came to this place; her parents had never lived in one place for longer than two years.

'You'll wear it out looking at it.' The gruff voice made her jump and she laughed. It was something he had said many times and she knew he understood.

John McQuillan was wearing his best suit and looked distinguished, his skin weather-beaten, his hair dark with silvered streaks. He prepared to help her, smiling as he heard the excited voices of the children coming from the lounge.

'If only life was a party, eh?' He saw by her profile he had interpreted some of her thoughts. 'You're a sensible lass, Scarlett; I know you'll try and give Ross a fair deal.' Her eyes told him she didn't expect the same from his son and he smiled ruefully.

'You're right to be wary. He's not in a state of mind to make commitments and, much as I love him, I don't want to see you hurt again.'

'Thank you.' She was touched, surprised to find for the second time that evening that the McQuillans did consider and understand some of her feelings on the matter.

She endured the festivities until nine o'clock, when she considered it was time she took Jordan home. She attempted to avoid Ross but Jordan wanted to say goodbye to him. Ross immediately volunteered to drive her the short distance home.

'It's a fine night.' She tried to put him off. 'We can walk.'

'You must be joking.' His mouth firmed into a hard line. 'It's nearly a mile down that track. I can't believe it's common practice for you to walk alone.'

'I always ring.'

'Scarlett values her independence,' Mary informed him with a hint of disapproval neither missed.

'Scarlett gets her own way too much,' Ross growled under his breath.

'It's a bit late to act the heavy husband,' she sniped at him, squashing her irritation as Jordan dragged his cousin Barry into view.

'Can Barry come home with us, Mum? Aunty Jeanette said I had to ask you.'

'Yes, if he wants to.' The more the merrier if Ross was to accompany her. Privacy she deemed impossible with the two of them in tow.

The necessity to talk to Ross negated by the childish chatter coming from the back seat, Scarlett reflected on her predicament. It was a no-win situation as far as she was concerned. Ross, as usual, would go all out for what he wanted with the considerable energy he possessed. She would have the fight of her life on her hands and if she were foolish enough to give in, which she wouldn't, she affirmed hardily, he was quite likely in six months or a year's time to find another damsel in distress and desert her all over again.

'Are you staying with us, Dad?' Jordan's question made Scarlett's head shoot round.

Meeting the mortification in her eyes, Ross smiled. 'Not tonight. I'll come back for breakfast.'

'Barry's daddy sleeps with his mummy,' Jordan piped up. 'You've got a big bed, haven't you, Mum?'

'I take up a lot of room.' Ross laughed, his white teeth startlingly white against his deeply tanned skin.

'Say goodbye to Daddy, Jordan,' Scarlett instructed feelingly as the car drew up outside the gatehouse. She didn't find the situation amusing, nor did she like the fact that he was using Jordan to invite himself to the house.

The boys hung around, finding Ross an intriguing addition to the family. Barry copied everything Jordan did, being a year younger, and he was impressed by the mysterious Ross McQuillan who had turned up like a character from an adventure story. Scarlett felt that the honeymoon period might well be over at breakfast; the boys in a less affable mood were going to take some getting used to on Ross's part.

'Breakfast?' he asked. She raised an eyebrow, having told Jordan to take Barry up to his bedroom with his bag.

'We have breakfast at seven-thirty; Jordan never sleeps late.'

'I'm going to help out on the farm; that won't be a problem.' His eyes were black and unreadable. 'Why, will you have to cancel your boyfriend?'

'I don't intend to cancel anything for you.' She spoke in an even, controlled tone. 'I could do with a lie-in. It's nice of you to offer to make the children's breakfast. It will help you to get to know them. They have cereal and toast.'

A slow smile curled his mouth and then he laughed softly. 'Make a fight of it by all means. What do you have? I'll bring it up to you.'

'I don't eat breakfast,' she returned pointedly. 'Goodnight, Ross.'

'Goodnight, darling.' His voice was soft and caressing.

Scarlett shut the door hastily as if to keep him and his words out of the house. Leaning with her back against the door, her breasts heaved as she tried to steady her breathing. Childish giggles came from the landing and she looked up to see two cheeky faces looking down at her.

'He called you darling.' Jordan went into a paroxysm of laughter, having reached the age when any degree of soppiness elicited a similar response.

'Have you washed your face yet?' she responded, seeing the tell-tale tide of chocolate cake ringing her son's mouth.

Marching up the stairs, she marshalled them both through their night-time routine, tucked them in and told them a story before she contemplated what she'd like to call Ross. Nothing as benevolent as 'darling' came to mind!

World War Three broke out the next morning. Scarlett showered after letting Ross into the house. She had been tempted to dress before he arrived but, deciding that she would keep to her usual schedule, she made sure her dressing-gown was secured and didn't linger long enough to provoke any masculine interest.

It started amicably enough. The boys were excited and Ross was quite capable of making toast. Of course, he couldn't be expected to know the possibilities of an unopened box of cereal. She trusted he wouldn't have any need to dispose of any rubbish and find the one she had thrown away.

At first it was the usual rumpus over possession. The plastic toy that had been added as a lure to children shouldn't really arrive in the cereal bowl until nearly three-quarters of the packet had been eaten. They were always, in her experience, down at the bottom. However, the boys rarely waited for chance to take its course and could be arm-deep in the box before you blinked. She had devised a scheme of keeping track of who had had the last one and fished them out herself before they had a chance to decimate the box.

Chuckling, she heard Ross's voice increase in volume and decided breakfast was proving more of a hurdle than the Lego castle. It was a pleasant change, she ruminated, to be aloof from the minor controversies of the breakfast-table and she dressed with a similar lack of haste, choosing jeans, a mustard-coloured sweatshirt and suede ankle boots, determined to keep her legs covered. Tying her hair back into a ponytail, she gave herself a brief glance in the mirror before descending the stairs.

Calm had been restored. Jordan and Barry were sitting in subdued silence eating their toast, the box of cereal nowhere to be seen. Ross was leisurely enjoying a mug of tea, the glint in his eyes suggesting he knew he'd been set up.

'If you want cereal, it's in the bin with the other box.'

Scarlett bit her lip, trying not to laugh. With a brief depression of her mouth, she commiserated with her offspring.

'He's got the spaceship in his pocket. It was my turn, wasn't it, Mummy?' Jordan pressed.

'It's up to your father what he does with it. From the noise, I don't think either of you deserves it.'

'My sentiments exactly.' Ross directed a retributive glance at her. 'At least we agree on something.'

Scarlett poured herself a cup of tea. With the matter of the spaceship decided, it was unsettling sharing the breakfast-table with him. Dressed in grey cords and a thick knit jumper, he exuded outdoors, and she guessed he had been out with John McQuillan at the crack of dawn.

'Dad says you've opened a café in Whitby. You didn't have to work; what made you go into that line of business?'

'I wanted something of my own.' She met his eyes steadily. 'I'm only an honorary McQuillan; I don't much like living on handouts.'

'You were entitled to use my money.'

'For Jordan, maybe.' She met his eyes squarely. 'I didn't feel justified using it for myself.'

'I'd like to know why.' He frowned as if the issue of her financial state troubled him. 'Can I see you today?' His dark eyes flicked over the children. 'Alone.'

'I'm at the café all day. Call in after three; it gets quieter then.' She had no intention of being alone with him; the bustle of the café with Tracy in attendance would suit her purpose.

He didn't comment but he didn't agree either, which made her nervous.

'Who picks the children up?'

'Jeanette.'

'Sounds as if you've got everything covered.'

'I acknowledge my responsibilities.' She couldn't help the gibe.

'Of course you do.' Ross regarded her with something akin to dislike. Glancing at his watch, he stood up, picking up his jacket. 'I'll see you later. Bye, Jordan—Barry.'

'Say goodbye,' she prompted the two mutinous faces. They complied begrudingly. Ross regarded the scene and a wry smile touched his mouth. He left without another word and Scarlett felt a shade guilty. Perhaps the cereal business had been a bit mean.

'Daddy didn't know it was my turn.' Jordan was aggrieved.

'Daddy doesn't know a lot of things. He's been away a long time.' Scarlett found herself defending him. 'After the nice toys he gave you last night, I think you've both been very badly behaved squabbling over a bit of plastic.'

Jordan's lip wobbled. 'Won't he like us?'

'Of course he likes you. I love you but it doesn't stop me telling you off when you've been naughty. Now come on.' She stood up. 'Aunt Jeanette will be here soon.'

They both went and picked up their coats. She gave them an apple each, bending down to give each a hug. Jordan clung a bit, which meant he was a little unsure of the new addition to their world. The box of cereal had definitely been a mistake and she realised why Ross had mocked her when she'd talked of responsibility. She had been so busy trying to make him uncomfortable, she had momentarily forgotten Jordan and his cousin. By the time her sister-in-law picked them up, she was feeling thoroughly ashamed of herself.

Saturday was always busy. There were a lot of fillings to slice and prepare for the Saturday hikers. Ramblers specialised in ramblers' picnics—hence its name. It would be easier for all concerned if she made up the rolls and put them in the freezer but she considered the food lost its taste that way, so came in early to make them up on Saturday morning. Saturday nights, Jordan stayed over at the farm. The Saturday-night stays had started off when the gatehouse had suffered storm damage and Jordan had gone there out of necessity. He had begged to be allowed to stay the following week, enjoying being indulged by his grandparents, and as it gave Scarlett one night of the week to herself she had acquiesced to popular pressure. Usually, she went somewhere with Philip but she knew he was covering for one of his partner's holidays and would be working that night.

Tracy greeted her cheerily when she entered the shop, eager for news of Ross's first night home. Scarlett sketched a night of family harmony, not going into the content of Ross's unwelcome attention.

'Is he just like you remember?' Tracy sensed she was getting a very superficial version of events.

'The very same,' she muttered hardily. 'He might drop in this afternoon. Will you cover for me if he does? I did say after three.'

'Yes, of course.' Tracy appeared to view Ross's appearance with relish.

Three o'clock came and went, leaving Scarlett with the odd feeling that she'd been stood up on a date. Tracy kept glancing at her to see if she minded and her irritation grew as the clock ticked around to five. She had sensed his reserve when she had mentioned meeting at the café but if he hadn't liked the idea why hadn't he suggested something else?

'He's probably been held up.' Tracy tried to make things better and Scarlett gave her an irritated look.

'It wasn't a definite arrangement. He probably decided to give Jeanette a rest and took the boys out somewhere. They had a bit of a misunderstanding this morning—well, they were badly behaved and he shouted at them. He probably wants to reassure them.'

Tracy was round-eyed and Scarlett realised she must think Ross had moved into the gatehouse.

'He came over for breakfast,' she added hurriedly, moving away to put the 'closed' sign in the window of the door.

Calling around at the house, she discovered that Ross had gone with John McQuillan and the children into Helmsley. He was going to walk around the castle with them while his father visited an old friend.

'Has he said anything about his plans?' Mary McQuillan asked her, putting a cup of tea in front of her. 'I hope he decides to give up journalism; I couldn't bear to go through all this again.'

Scarlett gave her mother-in-law a sympathetic look. It would be totally unfeeling of him to consider anything of the sort but that didn't mean he wouldn't do it.

'No, he didn't say anything about his job. We were supposed to talk this afternoon but he didn't turn up.' She looked into her teacup to escape from Mary McQuillan's compulsive interest.

'Didn't he? I am surprised; he seemed——'

Scarlett's eyebrows lifted, her topaz gaze questioning.

'Perhaps he was trying to avoid a row. Talking never was your strong point, was it?' Mary McQuillan shook her head, viewing her daughter-in-law's beautiful face with reluctant admiration. 'You wanted him so much when you were seventeen and now when you're mature enough to handle him you're so determined to throw it all away.'

A closed expression greeted the older woman's appeal. At seventeen, discretion was a word in a dictionary. She had fallen in love and followed love's flame without heed of sense or pride. But now she was older and the scales had fallen from her eyes. She knew what glamorous attractions were available to Ross. He might want home and hearth at the moment but what about next year, the year after? She was doing him a favour. There was no going back. She'd grown up enough to know that she could never hold him.

Her mother-in-law sighed. 'When I married, we took each other for life; now it seems such a transitory arrangement. I'll never understand the pair of you; you both make such a mess of things.'

With these words ringing in her ears, Scarlett drove back to the gatehouse. It was ironic; when her godmother had discovered Scarlett was involved with Ross, she had been intensely disappointed in both of them. Now she heartily approved of them making a go of things. Life, Scarlett decided, was never simple.

Without a date with Philip to get ready for, she felt curiously flat in mood. She tidied up and returned the house to order. She had eaten at the café and, although that had been around lunchtime, without Jordan to cook for she felt disinclined to bother for herself.

Going into the lounge, she put a Michael MacDonald tape on the stereo system and stretched out on the couch. The music was high-powered and dealt with charged emotional situations and that was how she was feeling. With Ross, she had always felt at the mercy of her emotions. He still managed to wreak chaos despite the formidable barriers she had built up over the years. Philip brought calm. His life was ordered. He was responsible and cared for people. The fact that she had to share him with his patients wasn't the same as living with someone who always wanted to be somewhere new, somewhere different. She respected Ross's mind. He was highly intelligent, he wanted to seek life's wonders and adventures, but the responsibility of Jordan had taught her that she wanted a safe place for him to grow, not the knife-edge of the world where his father existed.

The doorbell disturbed her reflections and she pushed herself off the couch, anticipating Philip calling in on his rounds, and went to the door eagerly.

Ross helped the door open as soon as she freed the lock as if he doubted his welcome, and she cursed her own stupidity. When Ross had asked her to talk, no doubt he'd had the evening in mind, and she had relegated him to a chat in the café.

'I'm not interrupting anything, am I?' He went past her into the parlour and then turned and watched her come to the door.

'You're late.' She glanced theatrically at her watch. 'I expected you this afternoon.'

'I had to repair the damage you did this morning.' He wasn't prepared to ingratiate himself. 'Jordan doesn't think I'm all that bad after all. Apparently, there's some kind of system established I didn't understand.'

'Had you waited to be invited, rather than thrust yourself upon us, I would have been more accommodating. I think it's rather despicable to use Jordan to encroach upon my privacy.'

'Your privacy!' He was dismissive. 'I think you owe me a little more than access to Jordan, considering the fact that I married you when it was on the cards that the whole thing was going to end up in the shambles it quite clearly has. If I was prepared to work at it then, why is it so hard for you to do the same thing?'

Scarlett viewed him with disbelief. 'Work at it! Your idea of commitment was putting a ring on my finger and

I was supposed to applaud on the sidelines for such personal sacrifice. You were so involved with your own ego, I'm surprised you even noticed I existed!'

He laughed at that but there was no humour there. Deep in self-mockery, his laughter scarred her.

'You made a strong impression. Why else would I remember you?' His eyes held hers, steady and challenging, demanding that she remember how it had been between them. Captured in his gaze, Scarlett felt the heady enchantment of the past return to haunt her. Oh, yes, there had been something special there. A fire, which burnt out every rule. Nothing sensible or polite had halted their passion; it had sprung from deep, cataclysmic urges that had nothing to do with common sense.

'Don't tell me you feel the same about Philip Parker. From what I hear, he's keeping a low profile. Frightened he offends public morality, is he?'

Scarlett tossed her hair back like a skittish filly faced with a brute stallion. 'I don't think you've quite understood the message.' She was infuriatingly superior. 'Lust may fascinate an inexperienced girl but I had nine brief months to learn the price and six years after to reflect on my folly. I don't want you, Ross. And that's all it was, wanting.'

His eyes blazed into hers. 'As far as you're concerned, I suppose it would have been a blessing if I'd rotted in the Amazon. The poor widow being consoled by the eligible doctor is a little different from an adulterous relationship, frowned on by the community.'

Scarlett's emotions were in chaos. 'I never wanted you dead, Ross. You have no right to say that. It's just that we're different people now. I've spent six years getting over the fact that I couldn't hold you—I wasn't interesting enough and I knew that you saw me as a burden to your glittering life. Somewhere along the line it stopped hurting and I've found peace. I like my life as it is. If you're honest you'll realise it's best to start again.'

'Peace?' He shook his head in disbelief. 'You're twenty-four, for God's sake; you sound like a candidate for retirement. I can understand you wanting time for us to get to know each other again, but why the hostility?'

Scarlett stayed mutinously silent. She was being asked to confess her deepest hurt to the man who had inflicted it. The dark irony of their situation was painful.

He came to stand in front of her, his dark eyes surveying her with harsh criticism. 'I was looking at the family album this evening. You're still as beautiful as ever but the vivacity has gone; I wouldn't be surprised if you pick your lingerie to keep out the cold.'

Scarlett viewed him with hard-won patience, her topaz eyes adopting a serene quality that was meant to irritate. 'I agree. I'm a total waste of time. Why don't you go?'

'I'll go when I want to.' A hard, implacable quality made his features stubborn. 'This is McQuillan land and McQuillan property. You haven't gained your independence from me; everything you have is bought with my money. If you leave me, what will you have to provide for Jordan? You work all hours in that café of yours, with my family to bail you out. I could give Jordan a better deal myself and I'd fight you for custody if you even think of moving him out of here.'

Witnessing the sudden mixture of fear and pain in her expressive eyes, a cold smile curled his mouth. 'I'll drag Philip Parker's name through the dirt for good measure. Don't make the mistake of thinking you can handle me, Scarlett. It's women who tame men, not mothers, and at the moment I think you've lost what it takes.'

Scarlett's eyes closed as if the light hurt them and she put up a hand to ease a nagging ache at her temples. Tears glittered in her eyes as she focused on his dark, swarthy features. He was in a black rage and she felt the power of his fury batter at her shaken defences.

'Why trap us both in something doomed to failure?' she pleaded with him. 'Ross, listen to the pair of us. We sound as if we hate each other; how can we possibly make our marriage work?'

Her words didn't touch him. 'We were trapped a long time ago, Scarlett.' Reaching out, he captured a strand of her hair, smoothing the red-gold strands between his finger and thumb.

She felt her heart double its beat, suddenly conscious of how close he was and of the strength and pure maleness he exuded. He searched her features, totally uncaring of his invasion of her space—her privacy. His gaze held a brooding intensity as if she was something he coveted, separated from his possession by an invisible wall.

'What do you want, Ross?' she whispered into the silence.

'I want you to live with me.' He was abrupt. 'I don't want sympathy. I want my wife and child back under my roof, I want you back in my bed and Philip Parker out of your life. You can do this the easy way or the hard way, but whichever you choose I can promise you the result will be the same. Think about it.' He went to the door. 'I expect an answer.'

Scarlett watched him go, rooted to the spot. However was she going to respond to such an ultimatum?

CHAPTER FOUR

SCARLETT approached Saxonbridge on foot, her face reddened by the wind, giving her colour and disguising the ravages of a sleepless night. Ross couldn't be serious about living together again; he had been angry and in her opinion rash. Returning to Saxonbridge had been a traumatic episode in his life and had probably knocked him sideways. It was understandable. Perhaps she had been too busy defending herself to consider what he was going through.

Jordan was busy giving a bottle to Calvin, an orphan lamb, and smiled in welcome. As she ruffled his hair, her nostrils quivered at the distinctive smell of bacon sizzling on the grill.

'Dad's in the barn,' Jordan informed her, as if it was only natural that she would want to seek him out.

'The barn,' she repeated dully. 'Is David with him?'

'No. He's gone home for breakfast.'

Glancing indecisively at the tall buildings, she stiffened her spine and prepared to be firm but mellow in approach. The smell of dry hay took over from the bacon, a stray bantam strutting across her path.

The barn was dark in comparison to the morning outside and she narrowed her eyes, listening for any sound of movement.

'Ross?' she called out tentatively. 'Are you in here?'

There was no reply and she shivered, not liking the gloomy silence. In summer it had a warm stillness that had a totally different appeal.

She walked up an aisle of black plastic-coated rounds of hay. Six years ago, the hay had been in bales without its protective wrapping. It had been here she had first told him she loved him. It had been the only time she had said it without being mindless with passion... Squashing that line of thought, she jumped, letting out a yelp as Ross appeared in front of her.

'You—— You gave me a shock.' She bit back the appellation that would have put things back on a war footing. 'Didn't you hear me shouting you?'

Ross was breathing strenuously, a slight glaze of sweat on his upper lip. His eyes were black, fixed on her, the shadow on his jaw suggesting he hadn't shaved that morning. He was wearing a black tracksuit, the neck open to show a smattering of hair marking his bronzed skin. Potent sexuality hit her like a blow. Swallowing drily, she tried to think of something firm and mellow to say but her brain had gone into shock.

'Morning, beautiful.' Ross curled a gloved hand around her neck and pulled her into the warm arc of his body before she had time to marshal her defences. The heat of his mouth compared favourably with the chill in the air, and Scarlett trembled in reaction, her lips parting in automatic defiance, but nothing came out, except for a sigh of breath. His tongue briefly seared her inner lip before tracing the edge of her teeth, the abrasive scrape of his jaw, flooding her with erotic memories she had striven to keep tightly locked away. The kiss blasted her riven defences, his mouth firmly coaxing hers, unbalancing her as he lifted her up against the straining bulk of his body, his chest heaving with the slow drag of air into his lungs. The leather-gloved hand brushed against her ear, roughly twisting into her hair. Tilting her head back, he buried his mouth against her throat, breathing in her scent, drowning in the familiarity of it.

Scarlet felt her body quake under the passionate assault. Every nerve tingled, but the cold air that she gulped had a sobering effect and she managed to whisper his name in protest, shuddering with something near ecstasy as his mouth returned to consume hers.

'Break—fast.' Mary McQuillan's bright call had dived into an embarrassed mumble on the last syllable.

Scarlett pushed Ross away with horror, gazing at him as if he were the devil incarnate. Mary McQuillan had beaten a quick retreat; they were alone and Ross didn't look in the least repentant. Rather, he was watching her with a heat in his eyes that wasn't friendly, it was purely predatory.

'You seem shocked,' he mocked her, his voice husky and provocative. 'Sometimes I think I've got a better memory than you.'

'You surprised me; I——'

'You need surprising, before you end up in a bath chair drinking malt drinks.'

'I can live without your concern,' she retorted belligerently. To think she had come to Saxonbridge willing to be reasonable! 'You know what you're doing, I suppose, with all this public demonstration and talk about "chemistry."'. That still stung. 'Everyone thinks we're going to get back together. I suppose in your selfish pursuit of what you want it hasn't occurred to you that other people are going to suffer when our marriage hits the rocks for the second time.'

Closing in on her slowly, he let his breath out in exasperation when she took a step backwards. 'I think we owe it to Jordan to try. There's a strong physical attraction between us, and we have a child—we're even married. I'd say we had a lot going for us.'

'You'd say anything to get your own way,' she muttered, watching him as if he were a poisonous snake.

'OK.' He relented. 'Tell me why you feel the way you do. Presumably it's more than six years that separates us. This Joanne Williams, what part does she have to play in this?'

'Why don't you ask her?' She bristled with enmity. 'You used to work with her. I believe you were having an affair with her before—well...' She blushed. It struck her for the first time that in the beginning she had been the other woman.

'Before?' he queried.

'She's more your type,' she finished lamely, not very happy with the thought of acting as go-between on Joanne's behalf.

Even before she had fallen from grace with Joanne, the older woman had regarded her in a maddeningly superior fashion.

'Let me get this straight.' Ross raked his hand through his hair, his expression gritty. 'I was involved with Joanne and you came along and broke the whole thing up. Somehow this doesn't feel like guilt you're throwing at me——'

'Me feel guilty?' Scarlet laughed hollowly. 'I had a crush on you. I was upset; you——'

'Yes, go on,' he goaded. 'I did what? How old was I, twenty-seven? Are you telling me I risked my future for a quick tumble with the local nymphette?'

'The what? You were the first man I'd ever made love with!' She marched up to him, prodding his chest, fury darkening her eyes. 'That obviously came as a shock. I was too inexperienced to let you have your fun and make a quick exit. I was stupid enough to think I was in love with you. You told me to wait until I grew up and fobbed me off with an emergency telephone number in case I was pregnant.'

'Well, the way I look at it, I'd probably feel quite bad about the whole thing. If it hadn't been for Jordan, leaving you alone would have been the decent thing to do.'

'Decent!' She nearly went into orbit.

'Of course.' He was enjoying her fury. 'You were only young. It's quite obvious that you were too immature to form a lasting relationship. Either that or there's something else to account for your present lack of feelings and blatant hostility.'

'I—there's really no point in this.' Scarlett turned away, hugging her body as if she were cold. She was fevered, hot one moment, chilled the next. Something had gone badly wrong with her emotional thermostat. The last thing she wanted was to recount the past chapter and verse to her estranged husband.

'No point?' It was his turn to get angry. 'You possess the past and you won't share it with me. I want to give my son a stable home and all you do is dismiss me and my part in your life and Jordan's as if I'm not worth the time of day. If that's your opinion, I'd like to know why.'

Scarlett bit her lip. She felt amazingly raw about the whole subject, something which she thought had been neatly tucked into the past, emotional wounds healed.

'I don't suppose it's entered that self-obsessed head that I might find the past painful and not want to dissect it with you? Especially with you!' She turned on her heel to face him, red-gold locks rippling around her shoulders in a fiery display, topaz eyes glittering with tears. 'I was only a small part of your past, Ross. Nine months isn't that long to remain forgotten and for my sake I wish you'd leave it that way.'

Ross regarded her critically. 'But I haven't forgotten you, Scarlett. You're the only one that looks familiar—

feels familiar...' he smiled devilishly '...tastes familiar. At least with me you look alive, even if you are close to tears. Your friendly GP isn't lighting any fires; if you were passionately involved you wouldn't find my presence so disturbing.'

Her eyes widened as she felt the truth of his words wound her anew. Was Philip no more than a friend? He had kissed her upon occasion but they were safe, warm kisses. His hands never ran over her in that intimate, familiar manner adopted by Ross. His body never expressed such urgency and drove hers to the same heights.

'You're hiding behind him, aren't you? You're scared of loving and I'm going to find out why.'

'Why? So you can trample my feelings into the dust for the second time? You don't know anything about loving, Ross, unless it's when you're looking in the mirror.'

'You could teach me,' he offered, unabashed. 'I might enjoy that.'

'I'm sure you won't be short of offers.' She looked towards the open door, hearing the sound of approaching feet.

'You still haven't given me an answer,' Ross reminded her gently and her eyes flashed back to him as John McQuillan came into the barn preceded by Karis and Drake.

'Your breakfast's getting cold, Ross.' His father regarded him with a reproving eye. 'It'd be warmer talking indoors.'

'Oh, I don't know.' There was humour in Ross's eyes. 'It's pretty warm in here.'

Scarlett was the first to leave the barn, the fresh air reviving her somewhat. Calling Jordan, she made a brief, unconvincing excuse that they were to visit friends and preceded her complaining son along the track leading to the gatehouse.

Everything seemed determined to plot against her. Ross was pursuing her, Jordan was keen to spend as much time with his father as possible, Philip had virtually disappeared off the map and the whole community awaited a happy ending to Ross's exotic adventure. No doubt Joanne would put a cat among the pigeons when she stalked Ross to Saxonbridge but that idea didn't bring her much cheer either. It was like reliving the past in slow motion and she didn't know if Scarlett the adult had the recuperative powers that had seen her through Ross's disappearance and Jordan's early childhood.

Philip Parker rang her that afternoon, making his apologies, claiming pressure of work. He wanted her to have a meal with him at the Scarsdale hotel, expressing misgivings when she suggested an alternative venue at the gatehouse. She didn't like leaving Jordan two nights in a row. Not that he would mind now that Ross was on the scene but she felt her husband might make capital out of it, especially when he found out whom she was to dine with.

'I'd rather not come to the house, Scarlett. Ross being back at Saxonbridge makes the whole thing a bit problematic. I think we need to meet to talk about it on neutral territory, so to speak.'

Scarlett accepted this. Ross could turn up at the door and she didn't trust him to be civilised if he found her cooking a meal for Philip.

She rang Mary and briefly explained the circumstances, trying to ignore the silent disapproval at the other end. 'Going out for a meal with a friend' had been accurately interpreted.

'I suppose you know what you're doing,' Mary sniffed. 'Ross won't like it.'

'Does Ross have to know?' She bit her lip to suppress her irritation.

'I'll try my best but Jordan will probably let the cat out of the bag. Children aren't very discreet.'

Accepting that Ross would be acquainted with her date with Philip, Scarlett reluctantly informed her mother-in-law where she could be contacted.

Philip arrived promptly at eight, finding Scarlett as eager to leave the environs of the farm as he was. Ross hadn't been at Saxonbridge, which avoided one arena of conflict. She was seated in Philip's Saab pulling out on to the main road when the Rolls purred past them. Scarlett found herself shrinking in the seat, feeling sure Ross had spotted them. Philip didn't say anything but his face had gone red and she knew he was extremely uncomfortable with the situation.

The Scarsdale had a varied menu and Scarlett decided on the Wensleydale chicken *en croute* while Philip, after much deliberation, had the trout. Normally they would be at ease and chat about past favourites and what they should try. That night neither appeared able to make light conversation.

'Is McQuillan bothering you?' Philip asked with difficulty when their order had been taken.

Scarlett considered this and answered honestly. 'He isn't making life easy. Ross thinks we should try again for Jordan's sake.'

Philip nodded as if he had expected as much and looked very serious. 'I'd recommend the same myself, if I hadn't seen how McQuillan hurt you. I've only known you two years but you're still suffering at the hands of that man. What are you going to do? I'm getting a lot of comments from my patients; some have even asked for a change of GP. I don't like things being complicated.'

'I'm not wild about it myself,' Scarlett was stung into replying. Philip's conversation had been rather ambivalent on the subject of their relationship. The only thing he seemed sure of was that he didn't want to become embroiled in a messy love triangle. She could understand some of Philip's concern. Ross did have a high profile in the area and in the media. 'I'll understand if you want to stop seeing me. I can see that it could be embarrassing.'

Philip frowned. 'I'm not sure we need to go that far. If you put the separation on a legal footing and we had an—er—understanding, I could look for a job in another part of the country. When I'm established you could come and join me there.'

Scarlett went white at the thought, unable to respond immediately because the wine waiter brought the bottle of wine Philip had ordered. Take Jordan away from the McQuillans? It was unthinkable. Ross wouldn't allow it without a fight and relations with the rest of the family would be extremely fraught.

'I know it's a big decision.' Philip poured the white wine into her glass. 'But it has to be made. I can't see our relationship working here in Yorkshire.'

Leave Yorkshire! Scarlett winced inwardly. Saxonbridge was the only home she had ever had. Jordan had never known anything else and whatever she thought of the McQuillans *en masse* they were a warm, loving family who had given them both a great deal of support.

'I——'

'Don't give me your answer now,' Philip reasoned. 'It's taken me a while to get used to the idea. I suggest a cooling-off period where we both consider our options.'

'Yes, all right,' she agreed faintly.

Scarlett barely noticed the meal. She could have been eating cardboard for all she cared. The knowledge grew that however much she tried to deny Ross's involvement in her life his influence was everywhere. She had enjoyed her evenings out with Philip and had never sensed censure from those she knew. They had accepted that Ross was dead and had viewed her embryonic relationship with the nice new doctor with gentle approval. Not so since Ross had returned. The atmosphere had changed. She received curt nods from long-time acquaintances and had to accept the fact that dining with Philip was now seen in terms of cheating on her husband.

The Silver Shadow was parked outside the house when Philip's car turned on to the track and Scarlett swallowed drily.

'Don't get out,' she advised. 'He'll only provoke a fight.'

Philip didn't like the idea of leaving her alone to face the man. 'But surely, if I explain——'

'Explain what? Ross wants to make things difficult for us. How would it look if you went to work with a black eye?'

Before he could argue, Scarlett opened the passenger door and got out, shutting it smartly and making for the gatehouse. Ross eased out of the Rolls, walking slowly up the track as Philip rather hastily reversed. She heard him laugh as the car disappeared.

'Big man,' he mocked.

'Big man,' she echoed but the mockery was directed at him.

There was a silence, Scarlett trying to put her key in the lock, the Silver Shadow's headlights dazzling her. They died suddenly and she felt a cold shiver trickle down her spine. Managing to open the door, she was aware of him behind her. Denying him access was futile; she knew enough of Ross to be sure he would have his say before he went.

'Doesn't stay for coffee?' Ross regarded her, his eyes obsidian.

'What do you want? It's a bit late for a social call. Can't it wait until morning?'

'No.' He came into the room, suppressed energy emanating from him in waves. 'How do I know he's not going to come back?' Pushing past her, he went into the sitting-room, glaring out into the darkness as if he expected to see Philip patiently waiting for him to go. 'Maybe I've lived in South America too long; I'd like to beat him within an inch of his life.' He spoke between his teeth, turning to glare at her. 'When did you leave the Scarsdale?'

'Why on earth——?' Good God, he was checking up on her, making sure she didn't have time for a furtive spot of heavy petting in one of the back lanes. 'I don't have to answer to you!'

'Why not? I am your husband—something you find all too easy to forget.'

'Forgetting is something we have in common, isn't it?' she scorned him, careless of the threat he embodied. 'You conveniently forgot me and our baby when you flew off to rescue your lover from Brazil. Why should I greet you with open arms when you practically deserted me when I most needed you?'

There it was out! He had all the facts. Now he could stop viewing himself as the injured party and consider the fact that he had reneged on his obligations to her in favour of flying to the rescue of Joanne Williams.

Ross closed in on her, dark eyes glittering. 'Are you saying I carried on an affair with Joanne after we were married? I suppose you have some kind of proof? Because without it all I'm guilty of is rescuing a colleague in danger. If the helicopter hadn't crashed, I'd have been away a matter of days.'

Scarlett felt trapped between the certainty of his adultery she had lived with for years and the inability to prove her case.

'What's separating us is immature jealousy——'

Scarlett's temper broke, her hand whipping to his face, hitting his jaw so hard that her fingers felt the pain of collision.

'Don't you dare make it sound like some childish tantrum on my part! I knew you didn't love me. I was never good enough for you and your high-brow friends. They all thought you'd lost your senses marrying a—schoolgirl!'

'You're not a schoolgirl now,' he grated, grabbing her jacket and hauling her against him. 'And even then they must have understood the attraction, if not the sense in giving in to it. You're a highly desirable woman, even if that stuffed shirt you date doesn't appreciate it.'

'Philip——'

'Don't elaborate.' His voice dropped warningly, his dark face inches from hers. 'I don't know how any man could kiss you and not take it further. I've been thinking about you all day——'

'Ross...' She warned him off, her voice husky even to her own ears.

'You want me. You've just piled up all these juvenile grievances until they walled you in.'

'No,' she denied, pushing at his chest as his arms pulled her into his body, the jar of his lean frame against the softness of hers sending dizzy signals of delight throughout her body.

'You say no and your thighs melt against mine. Hard to explain, isn't it, Scarlett? That wicked little tongue of yours wasn't saying no when I kissed you this morning. If we hadn't been disturbed, we'd have set the barn alight, the heat we were creating.'

He could talk her into bed, she acknowledged frustratedly. Her blood was turning into molten honey and her resentment and bitterness retreating to some dark place, shouting with distant voices.

'Is this how you chat up your brief holiday romances?' She avoided his mouth, sending up a prayer for deliverance when his teeth caught the lobe of her ear and nipped erotically at the tender surface.

'They usually made an effort to get to know me. Do you like that, baby?' His voice was coaxing, the tip of his tongue teasing the delicate inner whorls of her ear, making her knees sag. Like it? She was practically jelly!

The second time he swooped on her mouth, she barely protested. Six years without the sort of magic Ross could conjure up suddenly seemed like eternity. Fires, banked down within her, broke free as his fingers tilted up her chin and his hard mouth consumed hers with devouring passion.

Warm and moist, his tongue ran over hers, creating an erotic friction that made her lips court his with instinctive sexual invitation. They ran through a gamut of emotions, their kisses warring, quarrelling and then soft, teasing, caressing with a stinging bite to begin the battle anew. Scarlett's fingers stroked the black hair knifing his collar, seeking the strong muscles at the base of his neck, lightly scraping her nail over his nape, and felt him crush her to him in response.

The couch was within easy reach and he pulled her down into his arms, lifting her so that she was trapped between his body and the back of the couch.

Touching the soft, pouting temptation of her mouth with his fingers, he viewed the feline drowse in her eyes and his own darkened dramatically. His fingers looked very brown against the white blouse she wore with the suit and Scarlett closed her eyes as he slid the buttons free with slow, dexterous movements, quite confident of her compliance. Brushing back the lapels, his hands were warm on her body, shaping her ribcage before gently undoing the front fastening of her bra, letting her swollen breasts free from captivity.

Scarlett's breath shook in her throat, feeling his lips brush under her collarbone, his tongue tracing the rise of her breast, rubbing silkily over the hard crest of her nipple until he took the warm jut of it into his mouth and held her squirming under him as he tortured her senses.

Scarlett felt prey to a thousand pulses beating throughout her slim frame until she felt the fire in her body could barely be contained. Her fingers strayed to his thigh, grazing the denim that covered his skin, feeling the contours of muscle and the strain of his arousal. He groaned her name, trapping one of her legs in between his and whispering against her mouth exactly what he wanted from her.

Some small part of her wanted to deny him. Was it because he was forbidden to her that Ross managed to ignite cataclysmic desire within her? His dark masculinity had always been a challenge to her, excited her. She watched him undo his shirt, her eyes compulsively drinking in the dark spray of hair on his chest, the line that disappeared under the waistband of his jeans. Shouldering out of his shirt, he took her hand and stroked it down his chest, gathering her up and shifting her underneath him, so that he could sprawl over her, his hips finding the harbour of hers, his hands pushing her skirt up her thighs.

'Did you wear these for him?' His fingers pulled at the delicate suspender, freeing her stocking and caressing her thigh roughly.

Scarlett bridled at the question. It was one of the few feminine fripperies she still indulged in but she couldn't imagine Philip being turned on by suspenders. How little they trusted each other came to her with startling realisation. How could he think she was dressing for Philip when she was virtually begging him to make love to her on the couch?

'I'm not a doll, dressing up for male satisfaction,' she spat at him. 'Let me up.'

'You've got to be joking, darling.' His voice was low with incredulity. 'Just lie still and I'll get you back in the mood.'

The blast of a car horn outside ensured that the mood was well and truly broken.

'What the hell is that?' Ross rolled off the couch, tucking his shirt back into his trousers, his body eloquent of his frustration.

Scarlett pulled down her skirt and tried to repair the ravages to her clothing, hearing someone enter the hall.

'There you are, Ross.' John McQuillan's gruff voice came from the door. 'One of the Friesians is having trouble with a calf; can you move your car so the vet can get through?'

'My car——' Ross swore softly under his breath, blocking Scarlett from view while she gained some semblance of order. 'Yes, all right.' Looking back at her, his dark eyes raked her with warm regrets.

He preceded his father out of the room and Scarlett followed them to the door. John McQuillan gave her a sideways look that held a glimmer of humour.

'Car like that can't be missed,' he murmured drily.

She smiled, a pink flush stealing into her cheeks. 'Thank you, John.'

'The vet can't fly, can he?' he commented reasonably, not admitting to anything. 'You might as well get in, lass. Ross can help me back at the farm; there seems little point in rousing David.'

Ross regarded Scarlett silently for a few minutes over the bonnet of the car and then shrugged, getting back into the Rolls and revving up the engine.

'Temporary reprieve, I'm afraid,' he said. John McQuillan waved the vet through and lifted a hand to Scarlett in leaving.

She knew what Ross meant. There was no way she was going to escape him in his present mood. He wanted her and now she had foolishly given him a taste of her weakness he would be back, hungry to finish what they had started.

CHAPTER FIVE

SCARLETT had never felt less like taking her turn leading the rambling club, something she usually enjoyed. She could easily have avoided the task, Ross's return earning her a certain amount of leeway, but she had no intention of mobilising her erstwhile husband as an excuse. Those who were cognisant with her visit to the Scarsdale hotel would no doubt circulate the news that Philip Parker was still an item. She would feel pretty shabby using Ross as a reason to beg off anything; in fact the way Ross was manipulating things, she was feeling pretty shabby about the whole business of her marriage.

Two questions pounded simultaneously in her mind. Could she and Jordan ever leave Yorkshire and set up life afresh with Philip Parker? Was she being immature refusing to consider Ross's suggestion that they should try again? Both propositions tied her in knots, disturbing her sleep and occupying her in inner turmoil during the day.

Jordan appeared in his waterproofs and hiking boots and Scarlett smiled at the picture he made. He resembled a miniature mountaineer and she knew, from experience, he would patronise the children new to the club mercilessly. Picking up her boots, she went to the door to find the Land Rover slowing to a halt.

'Dad and David are coming,' Jordan piped up. 'That's great, isn't it, Mum?'

Scarlett narrowed her eyes, spotting Barry as well and wondering if there was a family plot to have her brother-in-law watch the boys while Ross had another chance to harass her.

'Fine morning.' David grinned in greeting, helping his nephew into the back seat and getting in himself, leaving her to sit in the front with Ross.

It was a fine morning, the sky clear, the wind benevolent, promising to warm up nicely when the sun gained in strength.

'Hello again,' she muttered in an aside to Ross. He merely sent her a speculative look before starting up the engine.

Ross had certainly acclimatised quickly from South American climes. He had on expensive all-weather trousers in navy, a thick wool jumper and ski jacket. He would certainly win fashion points among the distinctly practical ramblers they were to rendezvous with. It didn't look like rain but that didn't mean anything in Yorkshire during March and everyone would be prepared.

'Can you read a map?' Ross queried as their conversation was drowned out by the noise of the boys chattering away in the back.

'Yes.' She sent him a hostile glance. 'I'll get us all the way there and back again.'

'And it won't take six years,' Ross finished for her, his eyes darkening.

'I didn't mean——'

'Of course you did. You just rather imply than vent your spleen openly.'

'Oh, shut up,' she said through her teeth, perfectly willing to be open if he preferred.

She couldn't blame him for the helicopter crashing, that was ludicrous. If she was honest with herself, what she really resented was the fact that she had nothing to hang the grudges on that she had nursed over the years. He frustrated her on all counts. She couldn't predict what would have happened on his return because he hadn't come back. He hadn't come back because of a situation beyond his control and when he did return he couldn't answer her accusations because for him it was all a blank.

They were to follow one of the Esk Valley walks. The route was well established, starting from Danby station. They were to climb up to Danby Beacon, nearly a thousand feet above sea level, and then follow a rough track to Lealholm. Calling the group together, she outlined the walk, conscious of Ross watching her with evident curiosity.

He fell into step beside her at the head of the ramblers, smiling as Jordan and Barry ran here and there like young pups off the lead.

'Got your distress flares and first-aid kit?' He was evidently amused by the oddments in her rucksuck. She believed in being prepared.

'We can't all get through life on a wing and a prayer. It would be foolhardy not to take precautions if anyone should fall and hurt themselves.'

'I stand chastised, Brown Owl.'

'Why are you being deliberately irritating?' She sent him a blazing look. 'I didn't ask you to come out with us today. You could have stayed in bed and given me some peace.'

'I'm rationing peace; you've had too much of it. Besides, it's disappointing to find the gorgeous creature in my arms last night has turned green and woolly over night. That's a most unbecoming outfit, despite its merits in the practical stakes.'

Red-cheeked, her eyes were hectic. 'I'm sorry, my leopard-skin leotard was in the wash.'

His laughter was a low growl, elementally sexual. 'When you were seventeen you were like a peach, golden and succulent. If you don't watch out you'll be a dried prune before you're twenty-five.'

'You're a rude, vile brute and I'd rather be a dried prune than feed your appetite.'

'Liar.' His voice softened. 'Last night suggested your body doesn't quite concur with that puritanical mind of yours. You didn't end up half naked on the couch for nothing, sweetheart, and I'm quite sure you went to bed aching just as I did.'

'I slept like a log,' she retorted militantly, glancing behind to find the following group rather closer than she would have liked, considering the conversation.

'Mum, you're going the wrong way!' Jordan yelled, sounding very important.

Scarlett, with twin flags of colour marking her cheeks, found it inconceivable that the party had nearly all missed the sign demarcating the route, if something absorbing hadn't taken their minds off their purpose.

Determinedly, she corrected their course and refused to meet Ross's eyes, knowing full well he would be amused by the situation.

Danby Beacon allowed them a panoramic view of the dales with Kildale to the west and Goathland in the east. High moorland to the south and the distant incursion of industry to the north completed all points of the compass. Here and there it was still possible to see crystallised snow, slowly melting as the temperature rose and the winds failed to keep the land chilled.

Scarlett felt her lungs slowly ease from the harsh climb, watching the stragglers regroup with satisfaction. She had tied her hair back in a ponytail but wisps had managed to escape and she brushed them back from her face, topaz eyes warm as she regarded Jordan, rosy-cheeked as he gasped instructions to Barry.

'Have you thought any more about our discussion the other night?' Ross asked, when they had once more established a lead of ten yards or so. 'I think we owe it to Jordan to give it a try.'

'And what if we fail? Do we owe Jordan that particular experience? He is old enough for it to hurt, especially when his relationship with you is so new.' Scarlett tried to evade Ross, feeling trapped by his insistence.

'I've thought about that. Why not come to Brazil with me? I've got to go back there and sort out something with regard to my business. We could treat it as a second honeymoon.'

'It would be a first honeymoon.' She was acerbic. 'Last time, we spent four days in London while you renegotiated your contract.'

Ross stared at her with disbelief. 'You're joking.'

'I must introduce you to yourself some time; you saw me as excess baggage, to be offloaded when unnecessary.'

'I should imagine you were necessary from time to time,' Ross returned, aware that she was painting him as black as possible.

'Not necessary, convenient.' Scarlett tried to stem the bitterness that tainted her memories. They had spent four days in London as she had said but Ross had been negotiating time to be with her during her pregnancy. It disturbed her when she realised how selective her memory had become. Ruffled, she changed tack. 'I don't need to go to Brazil to know we're compatible in bed but there's more to marriage than that.'

'I agree, but we've got to begin somewhere.'

'No, we don't. We don't have to begin at all.' She cast him a haughty glance, meeting the determination in his gaze and seeing the muscle flex in his jaw with satisfaction.

Refusing Ross gave her a certain bitter gratification for the pain she had caused her in the past but it resolved nothing. She was virtually living on his doorstep! If he grew tired of pursuing her, she would have a privileged view of his love-life, and she didn't kid herself that she was immune to that degree. The alternatives were either to consider Philip's offer, which meant leaving Yorkshire, or to try to find accommodation a little further afield.

'I'm going to fly to Rio next week. Think about it,' Ross offered, his attitude coaxing. It made a change from the unvarnished threats he had made upon delivering his ultimatum that she should resume her role as his wife or reap the consequences. Not that she presumed he had softened, merely changed his strategy. He could hardly coerce her into leaving the country.

Joanne Williams! Scarlett gritted her teeth. With TV crew not far behind, no doubt. She watched the woman get out of her Ferrari and sway into the Scarsdale hotel.

Instructing Noble to walk on, Scarlett tried to take an interest in the countryside breaking free from its winter chains. Nothing could distract her from the hot simmer within. It was as if the past six years had never existed. She should be pleased that Ross would have some alternative form of amusement but Joanne Williams brought out her possessive streak with a vengeance.

Stabling the horse at the farm, Scarlett discovered that Ross was in the study working. She took him in a cup of coffee, surprised to find him at the typewriter. It was all too prophetic.

'Joanne Williams is staying at the Scarsdale hotel.' She put the coffee down, not trusting herself to remain calm under the dark, mocking gaze.

'I know, she rang me last night. We're having dinner this evening. Would you care to join us?'

Scarlett looked at him as if she couldn't believe her ears. 'Haven't you heard? Three's a crowd.'

'I'm sure we can make Joanne feel welcome if we really try.' He deliberately misunderstood her. 'Besides, I think it would look bad if we both used the Scarsdale to flaunt our indiscretions.'

Scarlett bit her lip to halt the torrent of words building up inside her. 'If you need a chaperon, I'm sure your mother will oblige. Mary always got on very well with Joanne. I'd rather spend the evening with my son.'

'Our son,' Ross corrected mildly. 'Very well, if that's what you want. I'll handle the ravishing Miss Williams on my own.'

'I'm sure you don't need any help.' Scarlett was sarcastic.

'Jealous, Scarlett?'

'Not a bit,' she retorted derisively, wishing her eyes wouldn't betray her.

Ross laughed, a sound that trickled down her spine like a sensual caress. 'Which is why you came here, hotfoot, to inform me of Joanne's arrival.'

Scarlett summoned diminishing reservoirs of strength to appear blandly unconcerned by his provocation.

'Forewarned is forearmed. Joanne will be looking for publicity. After your last TV appearance as an emerging family man, I thought you might not want to be caught on tape cooing sweet nothings to Joanne.'

His teeth gleamed in a predatory smile, his dark lashes narrowing. 'You'd like Brazil. It would let that hot, spicy passion in you run free.'

'You've got me mixed up with someone else.' She turned on her heel, her spine stiff with pride.

'I know who you are when I kiss you. There's no mistaking the sting in my veins.'

Shutting the study door with deliberately controlled movements, Scarlett left Saxonbridge without encountering any of the rest of the family.

It would serve him right if she decided to go, she fumed. But the thought of giving him the satisfaction of two women locked in covert battle was enough to block the impulse. Throughout the evening, she brooded on the subject of Joanne Williams. She would bring Ross the world of TV journalism and witty, malicious gossip. A world littered with celebrities and dignitaries, a world in which Ross had enjoyed a high profile. Scarlett didn't doubt that Ross's talent and recent publicity would find doors opening for him to re-enlist if he wished. It was a world from which she had felt totally excluded.

The Silver Shadow purred back to the farm in the early hours of the morning. Scarlett watched it eat up the mile to Saxonbridge with burning eyes. Black rage howled inside her. How could Ross look at himself in the mirror? He was a pathological liar! Pretending to want to reunite his family and yet, at the very first opportunity, he was romancing Joanne Williams. As far as she was concerned, he had reverted to form and confirmed her suspicions. The knowledge did little to cheer her. Avoiding any contact with the farm, she spent the next two days pretending everything was back to normal.

Ramblers was busy, fine weather improving trade for the time of year. Easter was just around the corner and the town was getting its usual facelift for the forthcoming season, owners sprucing up the caravans for hiring to tourists.

'Avoiding me?'

Scarlett jumped and turned to see Ross leaning against the counter watching her as she piled crockery on to a tray.

'Hello.' She was determinedly polite. 'Tracy, could you serve this gentleman, please?'

'Gentleman? I didn't think I'd gone up in your estimation.' Ross smiled disarmingly at Tracy, who went pink and gazed at him expectantly.

'What would you like?' She grabbed her pad and pen.

'Some time with my wife. Unfortunately, she's not on the menu.'

Trying not to listen to his conversation with her assistant, Scarlett delivered tea and scones to two elderly ladies sitting at the far corner of the café that offered a view of the cobbled street. Gathering up used crockery from the vacated tables, she came back to the counter, her eyes steady as she met Ross's amused regard.

'I'm busy.' She was cool. 'Is it anything special?'

'I can manage if you want a break, Scarlett.' Tracy was obliging. 'It's easing off now, anyway.'

'Coffee?' Scarlett offered grudgingly.

'Why not?' Ross followed her into the preparation area, regarding the well appointed fittings and neat, clean work surfaces with passing interest. 'It looks like a sound investment,' he mused, watching her back stiffen. 'Is this as far as your ambition goes?'

'I'm content.' She put a mug down in front of him, eschewing the china she used for customers, and clutched her own as if she were cold.

No doubt he would find fault with her white overall and striped mint-green apron after the exotic figure-clinging armour worn by Joanne Williams.

'That's a rare quality,' Ross drawled, 'contentment. Something I've never had. Not that I remember, anyway.'

'You'd probably find it boring,' she retorted defensively, not sure where all this was heading. 'If you're trying to say my world is too small for you, save your breath. I've been telling you that since you appeared on my doorstep.'

'You've been fighting me with everything you've got,' he agreed, his dark eyes indulging in a lazy survey. 'But it's not working.'

Swallowing thickly, Scarlett felt her skin heat. 'Don't, Ross——'

'Have dinner with me tonight. We'll talk then, in private.'

'Jordan——'

'We're not short of babysitters. I can always come to the gatehouse if you'd prefer.'

'No!' She remembered the last time. 'I'll ask Tracy if she'll sleep over. She enjoys a night away from her family. She has four brothers,' she informed him inconsequentially, letting him know he wasn't getting the chance to attempt a seduction scene over coffee.

'I'll pick you up at seven-thirty.' His expression gave nothing away.

Scarlett sighed with relief when he left the café. He made the small, safe world she had felt 'contented' in resonant with danger.

Tracy was quite willing to fall in with her plans. 'I don't know how you can play it so cool,' the girl chattered away. 'It must be wonderful having a man like that chasing you.'

'You can't imagine.' Scarlett was droll, receiving a dig in the ribs from her friend that momentarily lightened her expression.

She gave in to impulse and bought herself a new outfit after work. She found a halter-necked dress that looked like velvet but was something much more practical. She had been considering black but the assistant produced a jade version with triumph. It finished above the knee and Scarlett bought it with severe misgivings. Ross would consider it a victory, but then was she going to dress drably just to spite him? Matching the dress with a short waiter-style jacket, she had merely to purchase a pair of black stilettos and stockings to complete the outfit. She drove home, feeling as if she had a guilty secret in the passenger seat.

Jordan wasn't too pleased about the evening's arrangements. His dark eyes were accusing. 'Why can't I come? Restaurants allow boys!'

'Not after eight, darling.'

'Dad could come here.'

'I've been making food for other people all day. It will be nice to have a break.' She knelt down so that she was on his eye level. 'I won't be late.'

Jordan gave her a hug and asked if Ross would read him a story before they left. She promised that he would. Conveying the request to Tracy upon her arrival, Scarlett busied herself getting ready. She heard Ross speak to her assistant before he came up the stairs.

Viewing herself in the mirror, she was surprised to hear giggles coming from Jordan's room. He'd certainly cheered up.

Ross met her on the landing, his eyes laughing, sobering rapidly as he viewed her appearance.

'Stunning,' he complimented, catching her wrist and viewing her with a leisurely air.

Pulling her hand away, Scarlett was arrested by the 'yuck' from Jordan's bedroom.

'He was a bit upset because he couldn't come.'

'I've solved that problem.' Ross adopted an expression of mock-seriousness.

'He's going to kiss you, Mum, watch out,' Jordan chortled, peeping through the door.

'Nothing more likely to put a six-year-old boy off his parents' company,' Ross advised her sagely.

Scarlett couldn't help smiling. 'Bed, Jordan,' she stipulated, wishing Ross didn't fit quite so easily into the role of father.

Her reasons for accepting the dinner invitation were mixed. She knew the present situation couldn't continue, not with Ross at Saxonbridge and herself and Jordan living in the gatehouse. She was also curious about Joanne Williams's visit and how that affected Ross's future. If he was tempted back into tele-journalism then Brazil was out and so was any slight chance that they could make a go of their relationship. It jolted her to think that she had been considering the trial period Ross had mentioned. She must be losing her reason!

Ross seemed to read her inner turmoil, his hand curling around her arm as he urged her down the stairs. He was looking magnificent in a navy double-breasted suit with a startling white shirt and maroon tie.

'Have a good time.' Tracy was breathless with the romance of it all, her eyes widening at Scarlett's appearance.

Ross courteously escorted her to the car, opening the door for her before walking around the Rolls to the driver's seat.

He had chosen a small, élite country restaurant called the Drovers. It was traditional, offering lamb, beef and chicken dishes with trout and salmon as alternatives. Old English recipes had, however, been thrown out of the window and delicate spices and herbs concocted a variety of culinary styles.

Chilled champagne was splashed into crystal glasses and Scarlett tried to reassert herself. He was being far too charming and that spelt trouble.

'You wanted to talk,' she reminded him, wishing she didn't enjoy his company.

'I want to know what your plans are.' He watched her carefully. 'I leave next Wednesday. Will you come with me?'

Scarlett lowered her lashes. 'It's not that easy. How does your mother feel about the trip?'

Ross looked irritated by her prevarication but answered briefly, 'She doesn't like it. But time will only worsen the situation; there's no point in delay.'

Typical, Scarlett summed up. What Ross McQuillan wants, Ross McQuillan does.

'I have Jordan to consider. And the café. It's not that easy, Ross—even if I wanted to go.'

Ross's dark eyes seduced hers. 'You're not the type to give up on marriage without a fight.'

'Our marriage is a fight.'

'We could make it a love fight.' He smiled into her eyes. 'Making up might be quite something.'

Scarlett broke free of his gaze, trying to quell the pounding of her heart. 'What about when we get back? Joanne probably gave you an idea of how the land lies with regard to your return to the media world.'

'What makes you think I want to return?'

'You used to find it exciting.'

'More exciting than you?'

'Much more exciting than me.' She sipped her champagne, denying the cold feeling the words brought.

'Joanne mentioned several contacts interested. Does it matter that much whether I return to my job or not?'

'It won't work if you get involved with the media. I know it won't.'

'I won't be dictated to, Scarlett. If you have any reasonable objections to any career move I choose to make then I'll listen.'

'Of course you will. You'll listen, put your case very eloquently and then do what you want. Just as you're going to Brazil when you know your mother won't rest until you get back.'

'Six years of my life are invested in that country. I'm not letting it collapse——' He cut the sentence short, his eyes flashing angrily. 'If you come with me, it'll ease her mind. It will do something for me as well——'

'Oh, yes?' She was sceptical. 'What can that be?'

'Not what you think.' There was an edge of savagery in his gaze. 'Through you, I can bring the two things together. The past, what I have of it, and the present. Even the future, if you'd relax and follow your instincts.'

'My instincts tell me to run and not to stop.' Her topaz gaze bore the demand of his.

'That's not instinct, Scarlett.' The candle flame seemed to reflect his gaze. 'You know what instinct is; we tasted the edge of it the other night.'

'Can we change the subject?' she stipulated in determined tones.

Ross held her gaze for what seemed like an eternity and then nodded, breaking the spell and allowing time to flow naturally again.

The evening was a cruel fantasy for Scarlett. Once, she would have died being the centre of Ross's world for such a brief span of time. That night his dark eyes caressed her, told her she was beautiful and flirted with her with wicked charm.

She learnt more about his life in Brazil. How he had found work at the Serra Pelada goldmine and earned his stake in a frontier town bar. He had kept Chad Mathews's name because he had no other and worked all hours to fill in the void of his past. Brazil was a country where the entrepreneurial spirit was allowed full licence. Ross had acquired two hotels before a partnership with Eduardo Adrade, a man from one of Brazil's old, wealthy families, gave him access to the capital to expand rapidly. It was a colourful tale and Scarlett listened with the rapt attention of a child. 'Just give me a chance, Scarlett,' he purred seductively, as she laughed at one of his jokes, her topaz eyes alight with humour, sobering quickly at his words.

'Time to go,' she enunciated in clear tones, glancing at the slim, elegant watch adorning her wrist.

'Coward,' he taunted lightly but gestured to the waiter for the bill and when he'd signed for the meal led the way out of the restaurant.

Scarlett gazed out into the dark night as they left the village and glimpses of hedgerow and stone wall replaced the lights. The car was a masterpiece of machinery, the Silver Shadow slicing through the darkness; it was well named.

'Last year, an old woman came to the hotel, bothering the customers, reading fortunes, frightening the life out of some of them. I asked her to leave—politely.' His white teeth slashed the darkness in a grin. 'She said I shouldn't mock fate, that I was lost in dreaming myself. Lost in dreaming,' he mused, 'dreaming of you.'

'You've made that up.' Her voice was husky. Why did she let him get to her?

'No.' He slowed the car and she tensed as they parked in a deserted lay-by.

'Don't tell me you've run out of petrol?' Her mockery disguised her rising panic.

'No, nothing like that.' He turned to view her, his lean body lethal and waiting. 'You've got time, exactly one minute, to tell me you're coming with me on Wednesday.

I don't want to hear about Jordan or the café. Both of those issues can be dealt with——'

'He's our son, not an issue.'

'Answer me, Scarlett!' His voice hardened warningly.

'Go to hell.' She was equally angry.

'Wherever I go, I'll take you with me.' His words held a passionate violence that shocked her into immobility. His hand curled around her chin, forcing her face up to his, his mouth devouring hers in hard, hungry kisses that added wave after wave of shock to her stunned defences.

'God, you get to me!' he whispered harshly against her bruised lips, his tongue a burning brand over the throbbing flesh. 'I want a woman, not a petulant child; emotionally you're still seventeen.'

'You're behaving like an animal,' she gasped, to have her mouth taken again with a coaxing eroticism that made her lashes flicker closed and her mind swoon.

Darkness took the colour from the world, everything in monochrome. Her dress looked black, her neck a pearly colour, smooth and silvered as her head rested back, hair trickling around her shoulders.

Scarlett's breath caught as he plundered the vulnerable hollows at the base of her throat, his teeth closing lightly as if to warn her of his predatory instincts. She trembled, not out of fear of him but some deep-rooted response that surged up from the depths of her being. The bite turned into a kiss but she knew he had intended to mark her. Why wasn't she fighting? She clutched at his shoulders, trying to push him away.

'Ross?' Her plea was soft and shapeless. It did nothing more than draw that marauding beautiful mouth back to hers.

'Talk to me in a language I understand.' His voice was deep and rich. His hands released her seatbelt, which she hadn't had a chance to remove, and he drew her against him, pushing his seat back into a half-reclining position that left him room to have her on his knee without the penalty of being hampered by the steering-wheel. Kiss after kiss seduced any resolve she cared to make and he didn't relent until her dress was around her waist and her breasts tender from the heat of his mouth. Scarlett was shaking, fevered, her face buried into his chest, his shirt cool against her cheek. His heart thumped steadily against the wall of his chest. He was aroused but in control, which was more than she was.

'You can't fight me off with the flimsy defences you erect, Scarlett.' Ross brushed her hair with his lips, his fingers leisurely caressing her naked back. 'I have little taste for making love to you in a car but push me and I'll tear that lie you're living to shreds. You need this.' He nuzzled her temple. 'You need me. Come with me to Brazil on the understanding that we try to share more than just a bed.'

Scarlett quivered as he forced her chin up, her eyes hating and wanting at the same time. 'I'll come, if you promise not to treat me like this again,' she whispered brokenly.

Ross drew her dress back into place, triumph glittering in his eycs as he smoothed the material over her breasts.

'Very well. Now, that didn't hurt, did it? Saying yes is painless.'

Scarlett retreated to her own seat, her body alive with embers of fire. It was a torment to relinquish his warmth, much as she despised herself for admitting it.

Later that night, she stared sleeplessly up at the ceiling, her fingers investigating the slight abrasion marking her throat. She would have to speak to Philip. In the back of her mind she had known she couldn't take Jordan away from the McQuillans; he was theirs as much as she was—— Her heart lurched as she acknowledged the blindingly obvious. She had never got over Ross McQuillan; her feelings had merely been put into cold storage. Now she was a woman, she had to decide whether she loved Ross or whether it was merely a passionate obsession she had never had the time to burn out.

CHAPTER SIX

BRAZIL! Scarlett stepped out into the heat and noise with a feeling of unreality. There were several very good reasons why she shouldn't have made the journey but her path had been smoothed magically by all concerned. Even Philip had been wonderfully understanding, wryly commenting that she had always been too involved with Ross for anything serious to develop between them and his normal spirit of optimism had taken a beating since her husband's return. He had decided to leave the area and start afresh somewhere else.

Jordan had been quite cheerful about the holiday, indoctrinated, Scarlett didn't doubt, by Mary McQuillan's rosy-hued view of the trip. She had caught the words 'second honeymoon' in hushed tones on several occasions and her indignation had equalled her embarrassment. She hadn't agreed to anything! Scarlett had made this clear to Ross, who had accepted her assertion with a mildness that was extremely worrying. It might be her imagination but ever since the aircraft had sped down the runway he had looked positively smug.

Who are you kidding? she derided herself savagely. Ross was banking on candlelight and dark-scented evenings to seduce her willing body back into his bed. She had done little to discourage him from thinking it would be an easy victory.

Rio de Janeiro was their first port of call, famous for its Copacabana beach and the twelve-thousand-ton statue of Christ the Redeemer on Mount Corcovado. Skyscrapers abounded but managed to look striking in contrast to the mountain all around them, the granite strength of Sugar Loaf Mountain guarding the bay a physical reminder of nature among this human extravaganza of a city.

They left the airport in a limousine bearing an emblem that Scarlett was to become increasingly familiar with. A carnival dancer was silhouetted against a background of gold. It was a brief hint of what to expect from the city; as dusk fell Rio took on the glow and glitter of a fun palace.

'It's a dramatic country.' Ross spoke reflectively, almost to himself. 'We'll go straight to the hotel; I expect you're tired.'

Scarlett nodded but her eyes were glued to the window of the cream BMW. A babel of humanity existed beyond the safe realms of the limousine. She knew that there would be a considerable African influence but was fascinated by the variation of cultures existing side by side.

The Hotel Garimpeiro was a palatial, modern structure of tinted glass and sweeping geometrical design. The interior was opulent and the clientele flamboyantly wealthy.

'You own this?' Scarlett asked huskily as a flurry of staff appeared to convey bags and a handsome young Portuguese man welcomed them in accented English.

'Yes.' Ross was amused by her reaction. 'Loneliness can be productive. Carlos, is the meeting with Adrade scheduled for this evening?'

'Yes, sir. It is as you wished.'

'Good.' Ross looked satisfied, pausing just long enough for Carlos to welcome Scarlett to the hotel and assure her that her every whim would be catered for. Taking Scarlett's elbow, he urged her towards the lift. 'I don't intend to work much but I must arrange the transfer of managerial power within the group.'

'Yes. Are you sure? I mean...' she faltered at the hard set of his features '...it's been your life for——'

'Six years, I know. You're beginning to make that sound like a lifetime.'

'It's Jordan's lifetime,' she returned hotly. 'Sometimes it feels like when my life began too. I never had anyone before that——'

'Can we save your emotional outburst until we have some privacy? Most of my staff speak several languages and have a working use of English.'

'That's rich,' she muttered, 'for someone who discusses our marriage on the evening news.'

She was assisted rather firmly into a private lift and endured the peculiar sensation of the elevation as they sped up to what her instincts predicted would be the bridal suite. Determined to avoid conflict, she decided to unpack. It was only then that Scarlett noticed her luggage appeared to consist of an overnight bag.

Following her puzzled gaze, Ross explained with a blandness of expression she was beginning to read all too well, 'There's been a problem with some of the luggage. I expect it will catch up with us in a day or two.'

'Yours appears to have avoided mishap.' Her topaz eyes glittered brilliantly. 'You really do like things your own way, don't you? I expect there's a boutique somewhere in this twentieth-century monstrosity that supplies all your fantasies.'

Ross laughed, putting up his hands to fend her off as she advanced on him, anger making her careless of a proximity she would normally avoid.

'Naturally there's a boutique. The choice of clothes is yours. I'll pick up the bill by way of compensation.'

'I'll pay——'

'It's very expensive,' he supplied, flattening her protests. 'It would offend your Yorkshire thrift. I wouldn't look at the price tags if I were you.'

She made an impassioned sound in her throat, hating the insolent black eyes that appeared to be measuring her up for her new wardrobe.

'I'll get Carlos to send one of the girls up with a selection of the plainer variety, if you like.' His eyes challenged hers with a mocking gleam that dared her to dim her attractions in sackcloth and ashes.

'That won't be necessary. I can choose my own things, plain or otherwise.'

Shrugging, he walked towards the bathroom, shedding his jacket as he went. Ross was keen to acclimatise, leaving Scarlett to take in her new surroundings.

A huge four-poster occupied part of the suite, the headboard ornately carved, filmy material swathed in a canopy over the bed. A two-seater couch occupied the stretch of gold carpet that matched the colour of its brocaded opulence. Two armchairs were placed strategically, one near the window recess, another near a mahogany coffee-table. Oyster-coloured curtains toned in with the white bed canopy, flowers abounding in expensive vases, filling the room with scent. It wasn't to Scarlett's taste but she could understand its appeal. The bed with its silken cover would delight eager young lovers.

Her eyes strayed to the bathroom; hearing the rush of water, she swallowed drily as she had a vivid image of Ross, his masculine body covered in droplets of moisture being tempted on to—— Fanning herself, Scarlett laughed nervously. Her imagination was running away with her and consistently turned to Ross for inspiration.

Turning away from the temptation the tiled bathroom represented, she decided to visit the boutique while Ross dressed. She didn't trust him to attempt any pretence at modesty.

The boutique was expensive and elegant as had been promised. It was hard to discern the swimwear from the other items on display. The evening wear section was more promising. She selected a crocheted top with scalloped edging and a flowing white skirt to match. Just to confound Ross she picked up a lavish lace creation, as black as sin, that crossed over loosely at the breast and hung down in witch-tails around her thighs.

'Quite a contrast,' the young woman hovering attentively commented with a broad smile.

'It wouldn't do to get in a rut, would it?' she queried, a spark smouldering in her eyes that the assistant couldn't hope to interpret.

She chose a pair of flowing trousers and several designer T-shirts, gritting her teeth as she selected scraps of underwear. Finally, she chose some shorts and a lightweight jacket to match the trousers and left the boutique before she could be haunted by the colossal price of her shopping spree.

Ross had promised to ensure that she was kitted out for the more adventurous part of their journey that was to take them into the heart of Amazonia.

Returning to the room, she discovered that Room Service had delivered a tea-tray and she kicked off her shoes, poured herself a cup and sank into one of the armchairs.

A cooling breeze came from somewhere and she listened absently to the alien sounds of the night as the hot liquid soothed her nerves.

Ross came into the suite, dressed for dinner, wearing a white dinner-jacket, his black hair gleaming. An aromatic aftershave wafted to her nostrils. He wore energy like a cloak around him, as if he had absorbed the electricity humming in the air of Rio, the throbbing heart of Brazil.

'I don't know how long I'll be. I have a certain amount of negotiating to do. Do you want to have dinner here or in the restaurant?'

Trying to fight down a familiar feeling of resentment, she reminded herself that this wasn't a honeymoon and she should make no comparisons with the last fiasco.

'I haven't made up my mind,' she admitted without any attempt to irritate him, in which she was certainly successful.

'Well, if you decide to venture forth, consult the desk and they'll provide you with an escort. Rio is something to experience at night but I'd rather you did it with me.'

'Don't worry, I have no intention of emulating Joanne. I know my limitations.'

'You make a religion out of them.' He wounded her without trying. He was halted from any further assassination of her character by the arrival of the packages from the boutique.

'Can I see what I bought?' He pulled idly at one of the bags to have her up on her feet, her eyes flashing.

'Wouldn't you rather be surprised, darling?' she hissed between her teeth, only to see the fires of quite another battle flare into life.

'I'd very much like to be surprised, Scarlett.' Kissing his finger, he placed it at the corner of her mouth. 'If I'm late, don't wait up. I won't disturb you.'

'But where——?' Scarlett stared impotently at his disappearing back. She had yet to discover another bedroom. He needn't think he was sharing the four-poster with her! She had made her position quite clear.

Scarlett decided on Room Service, needing to unwind, and enjoyed a leisurely supper before retiring to bed. She was determined to stay awake until Ross returned so that she could clarify the sleeping arrangements, but the travelling and hectic days before the flight had taken their toll and she was asleep in a derisory amount of time.

She awoke the next morning to find bright sunshine in warm bands around the room, one across the bed with the power of an electric blanket making further sleep impossible in the growing heat.

She discovered Ross sleeping on the couch and found a moment's sleepy occupation in regarding the sprawl of masculine limbs. His decision to sleep there surprised her. If he owned the hotel, he could have his pick of the rooms, but then he had said something before about having lived in South America too long; his sense of machismo had no doubt found the couch less of an embarrassment than not having his wife under his thumb.

It had occurred to her that he might raise the tension between them by sliding into the double bed when she was asleep. He must have a decent streak, she decided begrudgingly, bending to shake his shoulder and telling him the bed was free in a manner designed to be non-contentious.

'Thoughtful of you,' he growled. 'Ring Room Service and tell them to deliver breakfast, will you?'

It seemed that he had no intention of taking up her offer and she watched him head for the shower before picking up the phone, discreetly placing the cover he had used out of view *en route*.

Breakfast consisted of freshly baked rolls with a selection of preserves and fresh fruit. She had been informed that an English breakfast was available but she never ate much in the morning and anything like eggs and bacon seemed too heavy to contemplate.

Rio in the bright light of day was a sun-washed city softening the soaring white towers that in a less benign climate would have looked ugly, the mountains girdling the city giving the place a paradoxical charm.

'Would you like to spend the day on the beach?' Ross asked, approaching the table in the window recess with nothing more than a towel clothing his lower limbs. 'That way I can get some sleep and sun at the same time.'

'Yes, of course,' she replied politely, trying to ignore the feeling that he considered her responsible for his poor night's sleep. 'Did you settle your business concerns satisfactorily? I didn't hear you come in.'

'You were asleep,' he informed her with a smile tugging at the corner of his well shaped mouth. 'Adrade offered to buy me out, and I accepted.'

'Is that what you wanted?' She was surprised by his abrupt severing of his roots. After all, his life in Brazil at least offered him memories; back at Saxonbridge he had to make do with the recollections of others.

He shrugged. 'An absentee partner is fairly unsatisfactory for all concerned. I can't commit myself to regular visits; it would put pressure on a number of relationships, don't you think?'

Thinking of Mary McQuillan and Jordan, she agreed. 'It must be hard for you, letting go like that. Won't you miss all this?'

Biting his lip consideringly, he regarded her through narrowed lashes. 'Frightened I'm narrowing my options?'

'No.' She was flustered and it showed. 'I—er—well, yes, I suppose so. It feels as if you're putting a lot of pressure on our relationship, giving up——'

'My life here? I've told you, Saxonbridge feels right. If you've ever had one of those dreams when you keep missing the path and end up where you started from, that's what it's been like for me. Even if things don't turn out right between us, England will still be my home. I'm not designing a web of guilt for you, so relax and enjoy the sun.'

She was glad of his diverted attention as his strong brown fingers tore a roll apart and added some preserve. Aromatic coffee in startlingly white cups tempted her and she sipped it with pleasure and felt a little of the tension leave her rigid frame.

Copacabana beach was a white curve of sand, playing host to a sun-glittering sea and a lace of white froth. Bordered by the Avenida Atlantica, the constant hum of traffic along the motorway wasn't exactly quiet but the heat and the toasted bodies created an image of sensuality Rio was famous for.

'Ipanema is more fashionable these days,' Ross informed her, 'but I thought you might like Copacabana. It has an added vibrancy but lacks privacy, I'm afraid.'

That was all right with Scarlett. She had no wish for privacy. Privacy meant intimacy and his distant attitude since they had arrived in Rio unsettled her. At Saxonbridge he had pressurised her mercilessly until her nerves were drawn as tight as a bowstring. She had begun to respond to him, however unwillingly, and now she felt their relationship had been put on ice, which made her, if anything, more uncomfortable. She had been on the verge of an affair, if you could call it that when the man in question was your husband; now she felt like a teenager on her first date, and hated him for it. Ross hadn't lost interest; it was there in his eyes and the sensual message his body sent hers, but he was waiting for something and she had the unpleasant presentiment that the next move was hers.

Scanning the beach as relief from her thoughts, Scarlett was taken aback by the amount of bare flesh on show. Sun-worshippers abounded, vying with each other for the brevity of their swimwear.

Ross peeled off his T-shirt and removed his shorts. He had definitely adopted the native tradition. Scarlett's eyes slid over him and away again, the sun's heat appearing to intensify and spasm through her body. Perching dark glasses on her nose, she pretended to be interested in the beach life around her but couldn't get the sight of him out of her mind. He represented a magnetic force of masculinity, a glorious display of hard muscle covered by bronzed skin, dark hair fanning his breastbone, a thin line marking his stomach. She could remember tracing that tantalising path with a teasing finger, feeling him tense and enjoying the passion she aroused.

Colour invaded her cheeks and she glanced guiltily at Ross to find him viewing two Brazilian girls strolling with a lazy, hip-swinging gait down to the sea. Their costumes were negligible and from the rear view they were all but naked.

'Do they wear more at Ipanema?' she queried tartly.

'No.' His white teeth flashed in a smile. 'Should they?'

'I thought you said Brazilian men were jealous. They seem pretty liberal if they don't mind their wives and girlfriends parading around in the buff.'

That made him laugh. 'It's all right to look. Take any of the warm smiles and inviting bodies too seriously—then there's trouble.'

'Oh.' She searched the beach for jealous lovers but the scene was one of somnolent lethargy interspersed with some healthy types playing racket ball.

'Is it too hot for you?' He supported himself with his arm, turning to view her slender figure still clad in shorts and a T-shirt. 'You can't be shy. I'm sure whatever you're wearing underneath is—er—respectable.'

'The sun is strong.' She ignored the dig about her bikini, feeling grateful when he adjusted the beach umbrella so that she was more effectively shaded. She hadn't had much of an opportunity to sunbathe last summer, since that was her busiest season in the café. It occurred to her that she had boycotted the sun as if that tawny gold tan she had acquired the fateful summer with Ross had been one of many aspects of the youthful Scarlett that had been forbidden to re-emerge.

'Make sure you oil yourself properly.' Ross distracted her from her thoughts, with none of the lascivious offers of help she had half expected.

Sprawling out on a lounger, Ross showed every sign of going to sleep and left Scarlett to anoint herself with sun oil and decide how long she could risk her skin before retreating fully under the shade of the beach umbrella.

Scarlett found the morning's sunbathing surprisingly relaxing. There was a lot to watch. A constant stream of young boys picked their way in and out of the beach dwellers offering cold drinks and everything else imaginable in way of souvenirs. Other, more privileged children ran about on the beach, overlooked by indulgent parents. Scarlett's thoughts inevitably turned to Jordan. He would be at school, she acknowledged with a pang. She wondered if he missed her or whether his head was full of six-year-old thoughts about schoolyard battles and what was for dinner. A smile curved her mouth and she sighed. Ross and Scarlett McQuillan, she mused, opposite sides of the same coin. Ross had a secure family background and had travelled the world. She had lived like a nomad until she was seven and then it had been boarding-school and other people's families with her own mother and father fitting her in, in between missions. No wonder she had abhorred globe-trotting and put down roots so deep that even in the exotic pleasure spot of Copacabana she was still mentally at Saxonbridge, thinking of Jordan. It might have been different, if Ross had made her secure, if he had never disappeared the way he had, but it took a powerful imagination to believe that that would ever have been the case. Ross hadn't wanted to be her security; he had seen her need for something solid and stable in her life as a weakness. It was hard to imagine that he had changed. He was at home in Rio, comfortable with the language, the customs; his need for home and hearth could only be transitory. She knew Ross better than he knew himself; he was convinced they could make a go of their marriage, while she knew that it would be doomed to failure, and would take little satisfaction from being proved right.

Glancing across at Ross, she discovered that he was deep in sleep, his features heavy and relaxed.

'Ross.' She touched his shoulder lightly but he didn't stir. It had been over two hours since he oiled himself. She surveyed his long back. Picking up the bottle under his lounger, she noted with a sinking heart that it recommended regular oiling in hot sun. Deciding against it, she went to shake his shoulder, surprised to find him watching her with mocking eyes.

'Lunch?' he suggested drily, sitting up and leaving her with the strangest feeling that she had disappointed him.

'Yes—I suppose it would be foolish to overdo things.'

'Very,' he agreed. 'What would you like to eat? Rio is like everywhere else in Brazil—the steak is excellent. But seafood is also a speciality.'

'Seafood sounds good.' She tried to inject the expected enthusiasm. She didn't really feel hungry.

Scarlett tried to avert her eyes as Ross pulled on his mustard T-shirt and then stepped into his stone-coloured shorts. The light shades provided a startling contrast against his dark hair and bronzed skin. She had already donned her beachwear, the snazzy lime-green shorts and T-shirt lively against her red-gold hair, her skin sun-blushed but protected against going lobster-red by careful timing and a good sun-screen.

'Ready?' He reached for her hand and loosely linked his fingers through hers, his eyes daring her to object. She didn't and was glad. It was a busy time of day and getting lost wasn't an inviting prospect.

The restaurant he chose spilled out on to the pavement. Inside, palms and ferns proliferated, huge fans making the interior cool and restful. Scarlet found that her eyes welcomed the relative gloom as a relief from the daytime glare.

'*Queriamos uma mesa, por favor*,' Ross said to the waitress who came to greet them. She appeared to know him and smiled in welcome.

'You have Rio at your fingertips,' Scarlett remarked, as they were seated and menus provided.

'Why do I get the feeling you don't approve?' Ross quirked a dark eyebrow, puzzlement behind the curiosity.

'I meant it as a compliment,' she retreated hastily. He read her mood with uncomfortable accuracy.

'No, you didn't, but we won't argue about it.' He acknowledged the arrival of the drinks, cold beer for him and fruit juice that Scarlett had asked him to order for her. '*Obrigada*,' he said to the waitress and returned his attention to Scarlett. 'That means thank you,' he informed her, 'just in case you feel like letting your hair down and get into the spirit of the thing.' Taking a swig of the chilled beer, he met her beautiful topaz eyes with an arrested expression at the pain he saw there. 'I'm sorry, but I get the feeling you're not enjoying any of this. This is one of the world's most fascinating cities and it feels as if you're doing penance.'

'I'm here because you didn't give me much option to refuse,' she reminded him, recovering swiftly, her voice as cold as the crushed ice in her glass. 'And I agree, it is a fascinating city; I'm still getting over the shock of being here.'

'So am I.' His mouth curved into a humourless smile at the shock he saw in her eyes. 'I never imagined you'd be quite so vulnerable, even after our tumble at the gatehouse.'

Her eyes spat sparks at him. 'Do you have to be so crude? Coming here has convinced me of one thing, if I needed convincing. You're just the same, Ross. You may be older but fundamentally there's little change. I know you'd like to do your best for Jordan but——'

'Stop panicking.' He regarded her calmly, satisfied to have blown her composure to pieces. 'Coming to Rio was about us, not Jordan. Do you want the lobster?'

'No, I don't want the damn lobster,' she hissed, swallowing her fury as the waitress reappeared, and had to sit in frustrated silence as Ross ordered for both of them.

'How am I the same?' he asked as they were left alone once more. 'I can still make your blood race, can't I?' He smiled at her with devastating intimacy and caught her wrist, his finger finding her pulse which was jumping as he had predicted.

'I'm angry,' she retorted hopelessly, and his gaze mocked her.

'What else is the same?' he pressed on mercilessly. 'I still want you; that hasn't changed.'

Swallowing hard, she tossed back her red-gold hair in an attempt to break free from his domination. 'You didn't need a cosy fireside away from the bright lights,' she fought back desperately. 'Oh, it might appeal for a few months; after all, finding Saxonbridge must have been quite a shock. You need variety, a challenge; you'd never want what I want.'

'And what is it that you want, Scarlett?' He rubbed his thumb against her palm and kissed the back of her hand before releasing it. 'You thought you wanted Philip Parker but he was dispensed with easily enough. I think you want me but you're too frightened to make the effort to keep me.'

'Such modesty.' Scarlett circled the rim of her glass with her finger, avoiding his interrogatory gaze. 'I suppose I want to be in control of my feelings. You can't give me that, can you, Ross?'

His laughter was soft and somewhat defeated. 'You want everything tame? No, I can't promise you that; I'd like to help you cope with all that wildness you keep locking up inside. That would be much more interesting.'

'For whom?' she queried limpidly, knowing that they would never agree.

'For both of us.' His answer was predictable but it didn't stop her body from reacting with violent prickles of tension. Remembering the brown suppleness of his lean body on the beach, she hoped he hadn't a clue how unbearably tempted she was. It was a vain hope, of course; he knew the effect he had on her and that was why he was pursuing this subtle line of torture, circling her and then withdrawing, urging her to follow.

'How would you like to spend the rest of the day? Sightseeing? Tonight, we'll go to a nightclub and watch one of the samba schools. That way, even if you don't want to enjoy yourself, you'll still be able to give authentic replies when we go home.'

Wretched man! Scarlett sent him a killer of a look. She had the feeling that the next five days were going to be the longest in her life.

Rio, of course, was world-famous for its Carnival. They had missed the glittering spectacle by a matter of weeks but the winning contestants were celebrated afterwards and one of the samba schools was exhibiting at the nightclub Ross took her to that evening.

It was something she would never forget. Scarlett could imagine a fraction of the power of Carnival when she watched the sheer verve and exuberance of the dancers, gyrating in their costumes of spangles and feathers. The rhythms of the music belted out by the orchestra were irresistible and Scarlett found her toes tapping in no time.

'It's one way to get rid of the calories,' Ross murmured, watching Scarlett's fascination with indulgence. 'I don't know about the feathers, though; it takes a sense of pantomime to wear them.'

She laughed. The sheer *joie de vivre* made it impossible not to take the spectacle for what it was—sheer glamour, childish make-believe for grown-ups. It could only happen in a tropical city, where the Atlantic was more benevolent. Such exotica in England would be sadly ridiculed by grey skies and squalls of rain.

'I think it's wonderful.' She sipped her drink, catching her breath slightly at the taste and blinking at the aftereffect.

'Caipirinha,' he offered. 'Not unlike a margarita; they use cachaca instead of tequila.'

'Oh.' She took the next sip with more respect.

Whether it was the caipirinha or the samba or a mixture of both, Scarlett actually began to enjoy herself. She had worn the white outfit, which looked elegant if a little bit inhibited. Ross wore evening clothes and created a suitable stylish effect.

Later, they strolled through the busy streets and ended up dancing in a piano bar where the pianist seemed to have an amazing repertoire of movie music. As the night grew later, the melodies became slower and more seductive. Scarlett let herself be drawn into Ross's arms, dancing close without her usual reserve; those around them were almost welded together by contrast.

'It can be fun, you know,' Ross murmured against her ear. 'You don't have to be disloyal to enjoy a change of scenery.'

'No, I suppose not,' she mumbled sleepily. 'This is very nice, thank you.'

'I suppose that's an improvement.' He tilted her chin, his dark eyes mocking but not unkind. 'Let's go; I can see you're ready to drop. Your turn for the couch, I'm afraid. I'd be chivalrous but I know you're the no-nonsense type.'

'I'm nothing of the sort; I'd be perfectly happy to let——'

She drew up short as a beautiful Brazilian woman led a crowd of revellers into the small bar and halted as she saw Ross.

'*Boa noite*,' she greeted Ross with a snap of her teeth that was unmistakably hostile.

Ross returned the greeting, and Scarlett couldn't fail to be aware of a hush behind them and the stillness of the group with the woman.

'*Adeus*.'

The soft dismissal raised a small conflagration in the woman, who flounced past Ross with her entourage.

'One of your casual romances?' Scarlett queried sweetly, as he urged her out of the bar.

'Adrade's daughter, Maria,' he informed her tonelessly.

A limousine pulled up smoothly at the kerb. Ross opened the door for her and waved her in. Recalling the woman's barely contained wrath and her powerful connections, Scarlett wasn't short of reasons why Rio could become uncomfortable for Ross.

'Maria Adrade seemed rather upset,' she commented into the suddenly tight silence.

'Did she? Maybe she's had a bad day.' Ross refused to be drawn. 'We all have them, don't we?'

'We certainly do,' she retorted with unsheathed criticism. 'Let's hope she doesn't rush into the jaws of hell in a fit of pique,' she muttered, Joanne's plight and Ross's heroic rescue firmly in mind.

He yawned, his knuckles shielding his mouth, and failed to reply. Scarlett viewed his averted profile with growing confusion. She had taken Ross's desire for reuniting his family at face value. She had thought him naïve and unrealistic but had never suspected ulterior motives. What could be achieved by bringing her to Rio? She frowned and then shook off the thought. It must be the hangover effect of numerous gangster movies set in the city. There could be a hundred reasons why Maria Adrade was upset. Ross had made it clear that there were consequences of romancing Brazilian women, especially of high family. He was a man who quickly assimilated the rules and survived by them. And yet Ross was all too human, she should know that; she was his wife for that very reason. . . .

CHAPTER SEVEN

THE honeymoon suite had been returned to its original splendour. Scarlett gave a cursory look at the bed, wincing a smile as she was given a pillow and the spare cover.

'This is luxury,' Ross informed her in an inflammatory manner. 'Tomorrow, things get a little more basic.'

'And what does that mean exactly?' She hugged the cover to her and regarded him hostilely.

'You're getting the whole trip, darling. A reconstruction of my past—what I know of it, that is. You could say we've started from the top and we're going to work our way down. I like a systematic approach. Tomorrow we fly to Belém. A beautiful city, another high for me, once I got there. Then we're going to backtrack a little. You have had your yellow fever and malaria tablets, haven't you?'

'Yes,' she retorted, hcr spine stiffening. 'If this is a lesson that beauty often hides corruption, it's a lesson I learnt very early in life. My parents had a penchant for looking underneath stones.'

He smiled thinly. 'You didn't appreciate the lesson.'

'I thought it only half the picture. We deny human achievement if we only dwell on the disasters. There's beauty and warmth too, and people wanting to help. My parents seemed out to undermine their own humanity, as if they were apart from the rest of the world...' She trailed off. 'I can at least respect them; they didn't trade on disaster to make a living.'

'And I did?'

She shrugged. 'If the cap fits.' She had been thinking of Joanne but wasn't feeling in a benevolent mood.

'I'm not trying to teach you anything.' His voice was cold and hard. 'Understand, maybe. From the moment we met up, I've had the feeling you think my absence has been some kind of indulgence. I want you to know what it's been like, not the success but what drove me to it. How it feels to be adrift. Perhaps your burning torch of injustice could dim a little to accept the shadows of life. What are you going to do to Jordan? Restrict him to a ten-miles radius of Saxonbridge? It won't work, Scarlett; he's a bright, adventurous boy and you'll lose him if you don't ease up a little.'

'God, you'll stoop to anything,' she ground out, throwing the pillow down on to the couch. 'And what's the cure to this problem of mine—sleeping with you? I did that before and it wasn't exactly a form of liberation.'

'What was it, then?' He came towards her, tugging his bow-tie free and viewing her aggressively.

'An immature crush.' She tilted her chin, her eyes challenging. 'I was seventeen, you were ten years my senior—old enough to know better, don't you think?'

'Undoubtedly.' He regarded her intently. 'But I'm still committed to making the same mistake.'

Scarlett felt something inside her clench and nearly shuddered with the force of it. That was it! Mistakes of the past. She had had her chance to redeem herself with Philip. The very relationship she had claimed she wanted. She would have been in control, her emotions safe and inviolable. Instead, she was in Brazil with Ross, fighting the very same desires that had nearly destroyed her six years ago. It was a disease. She might fight it but there was no known antidote.

'So what happens after Belém?' She tried to defuse the tension building.

Ross regarded her with a bland expression. 'I thought we might take a trip upriver. Then visit the mine. Serra Pelada. My first hotel was at Marabá, not exactly on the tourist trail but interesting enough.'

'I'm in your hands,' she returned mockingly, deliberately appearing unimpressed by anything he had to offer. 'But unlike others I don't get a kick out of being in the world's hell spots. Voyeurism is not my style.'

'While being an ostrich suits you perfectly,' he replied with equal spirit.

'We shall never agree.' She stalked to the bathroom, the thought of spending another night in the same room as him anaesthetised by her anger.

She didn't sleep. It was all right while the fury lasted but when she calmed down she had to cope with his presence in the room. It was like having a sleeping tiger in the corner—she couldn't forget his presence and relax. What made it worse was the fact that the couch was very uncomfortable. It was meant for casual use; she couldn't blame Ross for not wanting to resort to its dubious comforts for a second night, since he was at least six inches taller than she was.

The next morning she awoke after fleeting sleep to the prospect of a flight to Belém. Apparently the city had been named Bethlehem because the expedition that had founded it had started out on a Sunday. Belém had prospered because of its strategic route to the Amazon, the rubber boom confirming it as a city of wealth and elegance on a European scale.

Once they arrived, Ross seemed keen to embark on a tourist extravaganza. The desire to cruise the Amazon was apparently very much on the agenda of any sightseer visiting Brazil. Scarlett could admit to a passing interest.

Ross might accuse her of being an ostrich but she had been affected by various documentaries that pictured the destruction of the rainforests.

The birdlife of the Amazon was rich and colourful, parrots abounding, brilliant reds, yellow and blues all competing to make the most noise. Toucans watched their progress with feigned boredom and Scarlett was sure she saw a sloth moving slowly along a branch.

'It beats a zoo,' she said laughingly to Ross.

'It could be a giant wildlife park if enough countries were willing to fund it. The Amazon has enough resources to farm. It's an ecological disaster to slash and burn for today, when tomorrow will produce a desert.'

She acknowledged the truth of his words. She had heard the same frustration in her parents' voices when they'd talked about the absurdities of human endeavour.

'I dare say the farmers have to feed their families. The poor can't be choosy about how they earn a living.'

Ross nodded, accepting the point. It came to her with a slight shock that she wasn't overawed by him in the same way she had been in the past. That didn't augur a new state of harmony, however, for it wasn't long before they were at loggerheads again.

Their journey seemed endless, although Scarlett was assured that they had one of the swifter vessels. At first she had assumed they were to spend no more than a day on the ramshackle craft; the fact that they were to spend the night aboard was the first shock. When Ross told her they were to sleep out on the deck in hammocks she thought he was deliberately subjecting her to hardship. She had a brief exposure to one of the cabins and felt almost suffocated. She took the hammock beside him on the top-heavy boat that seemed ready to capsize at any moment. The food was rice and beans, the toilets disgusting and the scenery, hours before a source of fascination, now seemed a monotonous line of trees that stretched into infinity.

'What are you trying to prove?' she growled at the opposite hammock, struggling with her mosquito net and feeling like live bait.

'Work it out for yourself,' he returned, sounding unconcerned.

Scarlett had expected an elegant seduction; the reality was something else again.

Once she had got used to the chugging progress of the boat and the sounds of the night, the hammock's slight movement rocked her to sleep. Sleeping out in the open was a magical experience, the night air cold enough for her to enjoy the warmth of her cover, the air fresh, altogether different from the steamy atmosphere marking the heat of the day. It was a different world. Casting her mind back to Saxonbridge, Scarlett thought that anyone spending the night out in the open would be lucky to survive hypothermia. The thought had a potent effect on her. It was as if the imperative need for protective clothing was a lock on the mind suddenly opened. This new freedom seemed to make her aware of her nakedness beneath the nightshirt she wore, as if the warm tropics had suddenly reminded her of the woman beneath the clothing, the woman restless to be known. She fell into sleep with a heavy languor, as if she had been drugged, but all night she heard the noises of the Amazon as if they called to her alone.

Scarlett breakfasted on coconut milk, watching with interest as an Indian family passed their stationary craft, travelling in what looked like an extended canoe. The man and woman both wore Western-style clothes, their belongings tied up in plastic bags. Their young children sat sedately, not clambering about and threatening the dangerous structure.

'Did you sleep well?' Ross queried, appearing to have acquired a cup of coffee from somewhere.

'Mmm.' She grimaced. 'I could do with a shower.'

'I'm afraid this isn't a luxury cruise. I could get you a bucket of river water if you like.'

She demurred. The Amazon was a muddy colour, a primeval soup that she suspected of containing all sorts of bacteria. She managed to wash her face and brush her teeth in the bottled water Ross had purchased before they'd boarded. Feeling a little better, she tied her hair back after giving it a vigorous brushing and managed to stand the cabin long enough to change her underwear and T-shirt. Smothering herself in suncream and insect repellent, she chuckled to herself. No wonder her parents had left her behind. With her colouring and skin, she was a disaster without the wonders of the pharmaceutical companies. Setting her straw hat at a jaunty angle, she joined Ross in time to see a helicopter land near by the riverbank. The boat accordingly nudged towards it.

'Yours?' she queried, recognising the logo.

'It would take days to get anywhere on the river. Besides which, we're heading in the wrong direction for Serra Pelada. I want you to see the mine.'

'The birth of your empire?' she queried flippantly.

'More or less. It's picturesque in a way. It's certainly had its share of spreads in the up-market glossies.'

Scarlett could imagine. She almost expected Joanne Williams to be there to greet them, cooing about the atmosphere.

The trip was typical of Ross. They had flitted from Rio to Belém, cruised the Amazon and now headed towards the Serra Pelada goldmine in the time it would take most people to find a space on the beach and attempt to sample the delights of Rio. It fuelled her belief that Ross would never settle down. But Scarlett didn't have long to ponder on Ross's shortcomings as a family man, for they were soon on the move again.

The Amazon was dotted with projects of various kinds that appeared to be served by incoming helicopters. River and road routes were possibilities but time-consuming. Helicopters provided an excellent vehicle for bringing in supplies and ferrying those who could afford them to cover the vast territory.

Scarlett was surprised at the choice in transport but when she mentioned it Ross said that he had no memory of the crash and had been in such craft more times than he cared to remember. What little she knew of amnesia suggested it had an emotional base that was self-protective during times of trauma. Ross had forgotten his past, dusted himself down and started all over again. It was so like him, she wondered at her own surprise.

They spent the second night in a camp established by a mining company surveying the area's mineral resources. It was a male environment in the middle of miles of jungle. They had a makeshift shower and Scarlett overcame her feeling of self-consciousness, letting tepid water wash the accumulated sweat from her body.

They were given a thatched hut with a tarpaulin covering to keep out the rain. She needn't have bothered showering, Scarlett reflected an hour later, when the skies opened and rain came down in a deluge. When it was over, the atmosphere was similar to a sauna. Heat and moisture redolent with the smell of earth and vegetation permeated the air and everything was damp.

Ross seemed to thrive in the heat. His skin had a coppery sheen, his shorts and T-shirt revealing his skin in blatant invitation to the sun and insect life that abounded.

None of the men spoke English and she felt very much wife of the big man. The fact that Ross was so clearly respected made her feel safe. More than once, she felt male eyes slide over her assessingly. In the jungle, she felt the social games and rituals of nicety were swept away to show life at its basic level. These men weren't exactly starved of female company—but that didn't stop them finding an unexpected female visitor, especially of Scarlett's colouring, a novelty to be appreciated. Her intellect, it seemed, they were quite willing to forgo.

'You seemed uncomfortable,' Ross commented, following her into the hut.

'Unlike you,' she remarked, sitting gingerly on the side of her camp bed and pushing back the gauze canopy to gain access while she undid her shoes. 'Women exist here between the pages of dubious magazines, I should imagine.'

Ross grinned, his white teeth showing in the gloom. 'Something like that. The language barrier doesn't help when it comes to appreciating your personality.'

'Do women need one, I wonder?' Her tone was dry. She wriggled her toes and drew up her feet to stretch out on the camp bed. The atmosphere was enervating.

'My memory didn't stretch as far as your personality,' Ross murmured, following her example and stretching out on his camp bed. 'Not that it hasn't been delightful finding out.'

Scarlett turned her head sideways, too tired to respond to his provocation. He had his eyes closed, his hands behind his head making his biceps bulge. His T-shirt was damp and clinging to him, outlining the strong muscular contours of his chest.

Biting her lip, she tried to deny the stirring feelings of desire. How was she going to get out of this damn jungle without making the biggest mistake of her life? She had been ready to deal with the romantic candlelit dinners but not the heat, the lack of civilised plumbing and her own sexual drive responding to the fecundity of the jungle, making her blood sizzle through her veins.

Eyes as black as night returned her gaze. Scarlett had been regarding him drowsily and a sudden *frisson* of awareness made her blink.

'Tomorrow night we'll have a proper bed,' he told her, his voice low and gravelly, infinitely sexy. 'Until then, keep it cool, darling.'

'You...' Words failed her. Ross had turned his back and she was left, seething with fury, with nothing to vent her spleen on but the unforthcoming target of her husband's back.

Serra Pelada mines had provoked a gold rush in the Eighties that had seen thousands of men flood to the area hoping to make their fortunes. Some were still there. It was a hundred kilometres south-west of Marabá and not a place for the faint-hearted. It was frontier land reminiscent of the American movies dealing with the gold rush centuries before. The mines were in decline, Ross informed her but there still seemed considerable activity. Hope, she reflected sardonically, had little to do with logic.

The mine had all the features of a biblical epic, huge golden-grey blocks of stone dwarfing the men who swarmed over the hewn rock in an endless search for gold and a passport to riches.

'You lived here?' Scarlett echoed faintly, aware of his careless grin.

'Impressive, isn't it? I found a nugget the size of your fist and nearly got killed for it. It's a dog-eat-dog world, the only rule—survival.' He stroked a hand across his stomach as if remembering something. 'Would you like to stay the night, soak up the atmosphere?'

Looking around at the desperate faces in their stained shorts and T-shirts, she shook her head decisively, hearing him laugh.

'This place isn't exactly healthy.' He agreed with her judgement.

'I've heard malaria is rife in the camp.' She recalled the chatter of one of the maids at the Belém hotel.

'I wasn't thinking about malaria. Some of them would take the fillings out of your teeth, if they had any value.'

She glanced around nervously, noticing the covetous look she was getting, and felt her throat tighten. They made the men at the mining camp look like gentlemen.

'Relax. No one is going to harm you while I'm around.'

'And what does that say about you?' she queried, getting back into the helicopter, feeling it was a welcome sign of civilisation.

'It says I know my way around this particular jungle and take the necessary precautions.' He pushed a hand through his hair in an effort to cool his scalp, the dark strands gleaming with sweat. 'We'll go to the hotel in Marabá. That should soothe your need for civilisation.'

Scarlett was stung by his gentle mockery. Had he expected her to get some kind of vicarious thrill from all those tired, gold-hungry faces? Some of the prospectors were barely out of childhood. No doubt it was the seedy exotica of goldmining that appealed to him. The gamble on lady luck, pitting your wits against others with a similar hunger for life... She shuddered. It was undeniably a male world. Joanne Williams, for all her worldly sophistication, had needed Ross to protect her against the predatory laws of this jungle in all its dimensions. Ross, she realised, was not providing her with a series of snapshots of Brazil, he was systematically challenging her condemnation of his rescue mission and what that sacrifice had cost him. She gritted her teeth, tears stinging her eyes. He was removing her defences to win a prize he wouldn't value. The injustice of it made her bite her lip to control the pain.

Ross was thankfully unaware of her plague of emotions and was drinking in the sight of the goldmine set among the backdrop of millions of trees broken only by the river that snaked leisurely through them. It had been a long day full of bright colours and vivid imagery. Scarlett was beginning to think all of Brazil was an assault on the senses and was pleasantly surprised by the red-tiled, white-walled building with decorative terraces that comprised Ross's first venture into the hotel business.

'More your kind of thing?' he asked, leading her into a cool, spacious bedroom with rattan blinds and a revolving fan.

'Very much so.' Raw from her troubled thoughts, she played to his prejudice without flinching. 'I'd like a cool shower and a cold drink. Could you arrange that, do you think?'

'Certainly.' He was in a dangerous mood and she met his eyes feeling fairly bloody-minded herself.

'And if you could manage to disappear for a couple of hours, that would make things just perfect.'

'Only a couple of hours; I'm making progress.' Moving with familiarity around the room, he tortured her by his domination of the space, coming close as he passed to show her the shower. He turned it on and then moved to a small fridge and took out a chilled bottle of Coke. He poured the fizzy liquid into a glass and handed it to her, holding on to it when she went to take possession.

'Mind if I shower first?' His dark eyes were potent in a sexual language she dimly remembered.

'No.' She tried to maintain her hostility. 'Be my guest.'

He let go of the glass and watched her in an absorbed fashion as she lifted it to her lips, watching her soft mouth caress the glass, her chin tilt as the liquid quenched her thirst.

Licking her bottom lip with her tongue to catch a stray droplet, she handed him the glass, her topaz eyes provocative.

'Thank you, I enjoyed that.'

'Nearly as much as I did,' he purred, his eyes inviting her into a world of heated intimacy. Calmly, in an unhurried manner, he undid the lower buttons of the thin cotton shirt he was wearing.

Scarlett swallowed drily as he pulled it out of pale stone-coloured trousers, her lips thick and heavy as she made the expected protest.

'Auditioning for the Chippendales?' She couldn't keep the husky note out of her voice.

'Who?'

'A group of men who make money fulfilling female fantasies. You'd fit in...Ross!' She shrieked as he picked her up and headed for the shower. 'Don't you dare! I mean it; I'll go home on the next flight and...'

'And what?' he grated, putting her back on her feet and using his weight to force her under the spray. 'Cool enough for you? Or would you prefer it cold?'

'I'd prefer to be a million miles away from you——' She choked with fury as he ducked her head so that water poured over her hair, the temperature lowering as he had promised.

'Not the impression I got last night,' he panted, fighting her efforts to get past him. 'Your eyes were begging me. Ever since you got out of those shapeless outfits, you've been sending out signals I'd be blind not to see. It's driving me crazy, staying in the same room, sleeping apart; I don't know what perverse satisfaction you're getting from it but it's not what you want.'

'And you'd know all about what I'd want, wouldn't you?' she spat at him, her hair getting in her eyes until she forked it back impatiently with her fingers. 'Let me guess. It wouldn't be exactly the same as what you want, would it?'

Scarlett tried to push him away, aware that her T-shirt was sodden and clinging to her revealingly. Her palm skidded over his wet skin into the tangle of soaked cotton near his shoulder.

'There's no secret about what I want.' Arrogantly, he pushed her back against the tiled wall of the shower. 'And we've proved on several occasions that you don't take much to persuade. Stupid of me to want you to behave like an adult but I've run out of patience.'

Scarlett barely resisted as his mouth found and took hers in a kiss heavy with sensuality. He had rested his arms against the tiles just above her head, his body slightly arched, not quite touching hers. She could have slid sideways if she'd moved quickly and prolonged the agony for another few minutes, a night—maybe a day. Ross refused to see what was patently obvious to Scarlett. They were mismatched! Becoming lovers was a fatal mistake. But the need to quench the fire was irresistible and drew them into a passionate maelstrom that had a reason all of its own.

Water ran down Scarlett's face as Ross smoothed back her hair, his palm cupping her jaw as he came between her and the jet of water, finding the soft, moist quiver of her mouth with intimate intent. Everything was a mixture of coolness and heat. A fine mist surrounded them, barely detracting from the fierce passion that blazed furiously between them.

Scarlett felt him shudder and was surprised to find her arms wrapped tightly around his waist, bringing him hard against her. For a moment she was startled and tried to pull back from the mouth possessing hers but Ross coaxed her back under his spell, his tongue teasing hers into daring response. His body was all hard, uncompromising angles and she pressed herself against Ross ardently, her kiss as generous as it had been all those years before. There was only one way she knew to give to this man and it was this total absorption... total surrender that she feared.

She heard the noise of the shower recede as he reached around her to shut it off. The silence was deafening as he lifted his head and watched her intently as he took off his shirt, his skin gleaming with water, much as she had fantasised what seemed like an eternity before. It was a compulsive occupation to note the water glistening on the dark hair flattened back against his chest. His body was well developed, hard and tough, and the sight of him made her breath shudder in her throat. Free of it, his thumb brushed across her swollen lips, watching the pouting movement that greeted his touch before his eyes ran over the curves of her breasts revealed by her wet T-shirt.

Taking the edges, he drew it up over her ribs. The material sucked at her skin. She raised her arms in a dream state and felt him smooth her hair back and then slip the straps of her bra down over her shoulders. His mouth found hers in a soft caress, his fingers sliding gently under the silken fabric to cup her breast.

It was madness to let this happen. Scarlett's thoughts surfaced weakly, her skin goose-pimpling as he teased the sensitive nipple into a hard peak. She had dampened down the tortured longings of her body and Ross was turning up the heat in a way she could no longer resist.

Running her slender fingers through his black hair, Scarlett had a burning desire to have his mouth scorch her body. He was not alone stumbling through memories—she had a host of them haunting her at that moment. She knew exactly how she wanted him to make love to her and this teasing, seductive touch wasn't it.

'I seem to have tuned into your fantasy,' he breathed against her ear, and she stiffened, realising she must have communicated her desires to him. 'Don't go cold on me, tiger, I'm quite willing to oblige.'

'Ross, no,' she whispered faintly, as he plundered her throat and moved his mouth damply over her breast. 'Oh, no, please——'

Her hand slipped nervelessly to the belt at his waist, his stomach muscles flexing at her touch, his throaty groan making needless of passion prickle throughout her body.

Scarlett gave a gasp of shock when he lifted her into his arms and strode through to the bed, throwing her on the soft surface.

'Make your mind up, sweetheart; you either want me or you don't.'

Scarlett watched him as he freed himself from the rest of his clothing, barely shading her eyes with her lashes when he stripped down to his briefs and met her gaze, his own potent with hunger.

'Well?' He came over to the bed. 'Want me to get another bottle of cola and we could take it from there?'

Dark eyes wickedly reminded her of her act of provocation and Scarlett felt her cheeks redden, unable to deny that or the tight peaks of her nipples that greeted his light questioning touch over their silken tips. He was a highly desirable male, she admitted desperately.

'Yes?' His words reverberated against her lips, to find hers parting to caress his, her fingers fanning over his shoulders as he moved over her in one smooth movement, the hard probe of his masculinity teasing the soft portal of her womanhood.

'Don't make me wait,' she whispered pleadingly, perfectly aware of the dark gleam in his eyes.

'That would be dreadful, wouldn't it?' he breathed harshly, his heart thundering against the wall of his chest. 'I haven't got the stamina otherwise I'd teach you a lesson you deserve.'

Roughly he kissed her mouth, before his lips burnt a path down her throat, his hips moving against hers as she arched into him while he worried the stiff peak of her nipple before nipping the tip of its jealous rival.

Scarlett was fluid grace beneath him, her invitation drawing him in as Ross felt a barely remembered magic whisper in his blood. He expected to find warmth and a sense of familiarity; instead he was burnt by the sting of erotic heat that made him take and be taken in one swift thrust of his body. Caught up in a conflagration of pure fire, he met in Scarlett a woman who demanded everything that was male in him and gave him in turn such explosive pleasure that it took his breath away.

He lay against her afterwards in the honeyed darkness, feeling the soft rushes of air into her body, as her diaphragm panted under his. Heavy with exhaustion, he became aware of her fledgeling protest as she moved to ease the pressure of his weight against her. Reluctant to let her go, he pushed himself on to his back, coaxing her into the line of his body, her hair flaming against his shoulder.

'You make love like a dream,' he growled into the red-gold silk, trapping a strand between his lips for a moment. Scarlett's topaz eyes mirrored his own deep satiation and it appealed to his masculine pride to have given her such utter fulfilment. 'No wonder I had to find you.'

Scarlett heard his words without any sense of pleasure. She had always known that compatibility in bed meant nothing. If they hadn't had that, they would never have got into the mess they had.

'You're not sulking, are you?' He tilted up her chin, unable to stop himself kissing the tempting curve of her mouth. 'Why did you hold out so long? You're made to love.' His hands were warm as they swept over her body, one hand curving over her buttock before going on to catch the back of her knee and draw her leg over his thighs. It wasn't long before he had her resting full-length on top of him as he coaxed her mouth into soft, clinging acquiescence.

Later, when he slept, Scarlett listened to his even breathing, feeling the heavy, relaxed sprawl of his limbs against hers with a tug at her heart. She felt as if she was seventeen again, just as vulnerable and just as confused. A love fight, he had called it, but in that he was mistaken. Ross confused love with obsessive passion; the latter could be fed elsewhere. With a sigh that was half regret and half reluctant satisfaction she allowed sleep to come. For the moment, at least, she could pretend they had a future.

CHAPTER EIGHT

THEY visited the mine again the next day, Ross showing her the hut he had spent six months of his life in, sharing with two others. She walked around the shanty town with him, noting that gambling was a way of life. With what little money could be made from the worn-out mine, the cheap gambling dens still had a busy trade. If Ross hadn't acclimatised so well, he might have got back to Saxonbridge sooner, she reflected, and spoke her thoughts when she looked up from her attempts at panning. Squatting at the edge of a stream sifting dirt, she had had time to let her thoughts run free. Ross was sitting on a rock near by watching the activity around him.

'Maybe we all needed time,' he murmured reflectively. 'Made a fortune yet?'

'No.' She viewed her intent companions and looked up at him. 'It's a kind of fever, I expect, not one I share.'

He smiled at her and she had little trouble interpreting the intimate knowledge in his gaze. It gave her little satisfaction; she had felt languid and at peace that morning whereas Ross had been up at first light, apparently thirsting for the challenge of the new day.

'Our guide has arrived,' he noted with satisfaction. 'Most of the wreckage has gone now, of course, but the helicopter came down about twenty miles from here.'

Scarlett gazed at him stunned. 'You want to go back to the scene of the crash? Why didn't you tell me?' She was hurt that he should keep his purpose for coming back to the goldmine hidden. 'Ross, do you think it's a good idea? Have you talked to anyone about this?'

'I don't need to talk to anyone about it. You don't have to come if you don't want to.'

'I didn't say that,' she protested indignantly, conscious of the approach of their guide.

'Good. We can go most of the way by canoe. It will give you a chance to see some of the wildlife.'

Scarlett shrugged fatalistically. It was unsettling, this journey into Ross's past. She had guessed something of his motivation to retrace his path from success in Rio to the origins of his Brazilian experience but this was something different. She guessed that he wasn't using this piece of his past as a lesson for her but as something important for himself.

Their guide and canoeists were Indian. Ross, usually a physical type, remained uninvolved in the propulsion of the craft, his eyes fixed on the jungle with an intent fascination.

It was a long, sweltering day. The Indians showed them the spot where the helicopter had come down. There were still stray bits of metal rusting after six years. Scarlett felt suddenly cold. He could have died here, she realised, glancing at Ross, to see him looking around, his eyes blank.

Moving to him, she touched his arm. 'Are you all right?'

'Yes.' His voice was slightly off-centre but he nodded to their guide who beckoned them to a spot where the jungle appeared a little less dense. They followed and the next hour was a sheer living hell of toil and struggle as they pushed their way through the undergrowth. Their guide had a machete which helped marginally. What effort it must have taken for a concussed man to make his way to the Indian village then the mine could only be guessed at. The village had gone, the Indians who had lived there retreating deeper into the rainforest.

When they finally clambered aboard the canoe again, Scarlett felt near to collapse. She took a deep draught of the drink provided, finding its tepid warmth less than refreshing. She would have pushed it aside but Ross made her drink it, saying that she needed the fluid.

When they returned to Marabá, it was all she could do to drag herself into the shower and wash the day's grime from her body, and then, in a desperate attempt to keep cool, she donned a cotton cambric top and shorts set she had purchased at the Rio hotel. They were really meant for nightwear and she dispensed with underwear as she intended to sleep for the remainder of the day.

Ross came in, viewing her supine figure with a questioning eyebrow. 'Do you want to eat now or later?'

'Eat? I can't move,' she breathed, her lashes feeling incredibly heavy. 'I don't know how you managed that walk; you must be superhuman.'

'Desperate people can achieve miracles.' His voice seemed riddled with meaning and Scarlett's lashes parted to show a slumbrous topaz gaze roused by curiosity.

'Do you want to talk about it?' She pushed herself up, resting her weight on her elbow. 'What were you looking for out there, Ross? You've been...different today.'

'Have I?' Shrugging, he went to the fridge and opened a bottle of Brazilian beer, tilting back his head and swallowing deeply. Wiping the froth from his upper lip, he viewed her with shadowed eyes. 'I thought it might help...fractured pictures. Stupid, I suppose.' He dismissed his hopes with a carelessness that didn't fool her.

'You said something about that before.' Scarlett knelt on the bed, looking up at him. 'About trying to put the past together.'

'Not an unusual desire in the circumstances,' he derided, viewing her for a moment before moving away and walking to the veranda. 'Go to sleep.' He cast her a dismissive glance, leaning against one of the wooden supports, the slight breeze teasing his black hair.

Scarlett regarded his averted profile resentfully. He didn't need to say she couldn't understand. That had underlined every attempt she'd made to reach him when he was troubled. In their short married life, he had been very good at reducing her role to bedmate.

Getting up, she joined him on the veranda, her attention caught by the sun, an inflated orange ball on the horizon.

'I suppose, later, when you're feeling better, you'll want to make love.' She kept her voice factual and was rewarded by the sharpening of his attention.

'I thought you were tired.' He cupped her neck with one lean hand, his dark eyes searching hers.

'We've found something you are willing to discuss, then.' Scarlett let her fingers close around his wrist, challenging his right to touch her. 'I've tried to talk to you about this but you won't let me in. You're giving up everything you know to come back to a life you don't remember——'

'I know what you think about that,' Ross interrupted abruptly. 'You can't take the emotional heat. Is that why you want to talk about my feelings? Life outside the bedroom a bit too much for you, sweetheart?'

'I don't know!' She almost stamped her foot. 'You never damned well let me out. You used to treat me like some brainless idiot who couldn't possibly understand the grand dramas of your life out there in the world's trouble-spots. It's taken me a while to become Scarlett McQuillan and not just your wife. I have no intention of going back six years, so if that's your intention you can forget it.'

'Quite a speech.' He drank from the bottle of beer as if he hated it, then rolled it across his forehead, trying to capture its coolness. Surprisingly, he relented, letting her glimpse something of his thoughts. 'I suppose I wanted to take the bits I remembered and put them together—you—here, like an old Hitchcock movie, where everything fits into place.'

'I'm sorry.' She had felt that kind of desperation to make sense of things and could understand a little of what he was feeling.

'Life's too short.' He dismissed his moment of revelation with a crooked smile. 'You can't say you've had the tourist version of Brazil. Sensible people usually avoid this neck of the woods.'

It was on the tip of her tongue to say she had found the experience enlightening if not her dream holiday, when pandemonium broke out outside.

Scarlett blinked as if to clear her mind as she saw two of the maids from the hotel locked in mortal battle not more than five yards from the balcony steps. The rains that day had turned the area off the path into a quagmire and their feet and ankles were rapidly becoming caked in mud.

Ross said something rapidly in Portuguese to the manager who had followed the two battling woman and his laughing response was taken up by the chef, porter and gardener, who now provided an audience for the fray.

'Aren't you going to do anything?' Scarlett was incensed. How could these women provide this group of chauvinists with such a passionate display of temper?

A rich chuckle escaped Ross as one of the girls neatly turned the other over her hip and sent her opponent head first into the mud. The other grabbed her victor's knees and dragged her down into the slime with her.

'This is dreadful.' Scarlett moved from foot to foot in agitation. 'Ross, stop them or I will.'

'I wouldn't advise it; an English rose would——'

A subdued roar of exasperation escaped her and, regardless of her flimsy attire, she strode down the balcony steps and grabbed at the arm of the nearest woman, trying to pull her away.

All Scarlett could think of was that one of these Cheshire-cat male spectators was being flattered by this fight. Probably the manager, playing fast and loose with their affections, using his position and relative affluence to dazzle these young girls. That was the last thought she had.

Scarlett hit the mud with a thud that brought stars to her eyes and the sting of salt in her nostrils. For some reason, the girls appeared to delight in dragging her through the mud and then they left her like a beached whale as they continued their scramble, appearing to search for something, and then the battle began again. The next thing Scarlett knew was that a drenching torrent of water blasted over her and she was unceremoniously hauled to her feet and quickly wrapped in an all-enveloping towel. It wasn't until then, peering up at Ross with all the indignation that she felt, that she realised her skimpy two-piece splattered with water and mud left little to the male imagination.

'How could you?' she yelled at him, and was picked up and taken back to the bedroom with curt, abrupt movements and deposited back into the shower area.

'Don't come out until you resemble a human being.' Ross spoke scathingly. 'You could audition for *Macbeth* looking like that. Of all the hare-brained things to do——!'

'I suppose you would have let them kill each other,' she sniped back at him. 'Or do you get your kicks watching women writhe about in the mud?'

'You know how I get my kicks.' He eyed her darkly. 'Something I don't wish to share with my staff—all of whom—may I add?—got a ringside view of your particular charms. If I hadn't decided to sell out to Adrade, it's the sort of thing I'd have to live down at dinner parties the length and breadth of Brazil.'

'That's just typical of a man.' She cast him a malevolent glare, wishing he would leave and let her get herself cleaned up. Defending her position from a shower cubicle, her face and hair caked in mud, did nothing for her self-esteem.

'And typical of your high-minded naïveté to rush in thinking you were going to achieve anything. They'll be in far more trouble having ducked you in the mud than they would have been for merely letting off hot steam.'

'Oh, so suddenly this is my fault!' she yelled at his disappearing back. 'I suppose I robbed one of your friends out there of enjoying the fight for his favours. I do apologise!'

Ross turned and came back and studied her with barely suppressed irritation. 'They were fighting over tips. You were lying on top of the booty. The police here aren't necessarily the first port of call in such a dispute. Why don't you grow up and realise that everywhere in the world isn't as tame as the backyard of Saxonbridge? And while you cope with that one, try this. Not every battle is for the aggrandisement of some egotistical male.' With a contemptuous rake of her muddy form, he turned away and left their suite with a hearty slam of the door.

Scarlett was left with the feeling that she had made an utter fool of herself. That she had misjudged the situation was quite clear but what was more humiliating was the fact that she had revealed her prejudice where men were concerned so openly to Ross. What she had seen in those two female viragos was her submerged self in conflict with Joanne Williams. She had felt that she wanted to wipe that self-satisfied, publicity-seeking smile of the journalist's face with every vestige of strength she possessed. Such violence of feeling was something that bewildered her and it was the enactment of such a struggle that had appalled her to such a degree that she'd felt she had to stop it. Psychologically, she supposed she had been curbing her own instincts and had ended up starring in the brawl for her efforts. A small bubble of mirth came from deep within her that burgeoned into a full and hearty chuckle.

'Scarlett McQuillan,' she cautioned herself aloud, 'you get yourself into some pickles.' She almost felt sorry for Ross, having to put up with his past sins being constantly held against him, when he hadn't a clue whether they justified such venom.

Scarlett endured dinner, gritting her teeth at the wide grins that were barely tempered by her direct glare. She had made a mark for herself in Marabá; between them the McQuillans could take on legendary status in this frontier city.

'I expect you'll have the steak,' Ross was provoking. 'You'll have to build up muscle if you're going to have a career in mud-wrestling.'

'Highly amusing.'

His white teeth showed in an attractive smile. 'Cooled down yet?'

'You were pretty steamed up yourself,' she retorted, viewing him with an assessing light in her eyes.

'I find your sudden bursts of passion bewildering. You dress as if you're considering joining a convent——' His gaze rested meaningfully on the T-shirt vest-dress she had donned for coolness. The shade of turquoise-green flattered her colouring but it was buttoned up all the way, the neckline scooped, revealing the tan on her upper chest but adequately covering her cleavage. 'And and the next minute you're well on your way to pin-up status.'

'I didn't expect to get drawn into a fight. Besides, that outfit was meant for bed—I mean, I intended to sleep, you know that.'

Grinning at her discomfort, he turned to acknowledge the wine waiter, silent for a moment as their glasses were filled.

'We'll order later.' He didn't bother to consult Scarlett which made her eyes glint. Viewing her with a slight sigh, he took her hand across the table. 'I've been thinking.' He silently admonished her look of feigned astonishment. 'I thought last night we'd moved on a little but——' he shrugged '—I suppose I was confusing sex with a deeper emotional compatibility.'

Scarlett didn't reply. She thought his timing was lousy. If he had come to the same conclusion the day before, her sensuality could have remained dormant.

'Let's begin with the premise that I'm not going to get my memory back. I can't see we're going to have much of a marriage if you can't forget the past, Scarlett. Somewhere along the line, you've got to trust me.'

Her lashes shielded her eyes and she moved her fingers from his, resorting to her wine glass as a way of avoiding his gaze.

'Trust isn't something you can just switch on and off,' she offered eventually. 'If you want me to put the past behind me then you'll have to give me something to build on. As far as I can see, my slice of your life is going to be very much the same as before. You don't believe in a partnership, and I'm not willing to return to door-mat status.'

His disbelieving growl of laughter made her look up. 'Doormat? You must be joking. If you were I'd be frightened I'd lose a leg every time I crossed the threshold.'

Scarlett refused to be distracted. 'You didn't discuss the winding-up of your interests here with me,' she pointed out stubbornly. 'Or what you intend to do with the future.'

'The future, as far as you're concerned, being welded to Saxonbridge,' he commented drily. 'Am I to have some say in how you operate? I imagine prising Jordan and yourself from the close locality of the farm a Herculean task.'

'Well, naturally,' she frowned, not liking his way of changing the perspective of their argument. 'Children have to have stability in their life.'

'Agreed. But that doesn't mean there isn't some room to manoeuvre. It sounds as if I either stay at the farm or I commute. The second option has zero chance of succeeding, with your opinion of my morals and your own insecurities.'

Scarlett nearly choked on her wine. The man was really insufferable. At that moment she wished him to the four corners of the earth!

'Don't you have any doubts when it comes to a long-distance marriage?' she queried sweetly. 'Or have you complete faith in me?'

Playing with the stem of his glass, his smile lit small embers of fire within her. 'I'm sure if you were to stray it would be with another stuffed shirt like Philip Parker. I'd get rid of the opposition before you got round to holding hands.'

Ignoring his attempts to provoke her, she analysed the bones of his argument. 'You seem to have made up your mind about the future. What is it that you intend to do?'

'I'm merely exploring the avenues open to me. When I sell out to Adrade, I'll be a relatively wealthy man. The money accrued from the sales of my books will be made over in trust to Jordan and yourself. The least I can do is make sure you're both materially secure.'

'A nice pay-off,' she commented cynically, her eyes widening at the anger in his.

'It's appropriate that you should have the profits of the past, since you're determined to live in it,' he bit out coldly. 'My base will be at Saxonbridge, whatever I decide to do, so don't think I'm going to disappear conveniently. One way or another, Scarlett, you're going to have to come to terms with me. Either as a husband or a very near neighbour.'

Scarlett got to her feet, giving him a poisonous glare. 'Let's practise being neighbours. I'm sure you can find a spare room——'

'Sit down and behave yourself!' Ross grabbed her wrist and jerked it so that she sat down, tears of pain blurring her vision.

'I'm sorry.' He passed her a linen handkerchief. 'I didn't mean to hurt you.'

She refused the handkerchief, blinking rapidly, and finally resorted to the serviette.

'I had hoped we would have sorted something out by the time we returned to Saxonbridge.' Ross tried a reasonable tone, clearly trying to dampen the sparks of conflict between them. 'But time is the only thing that's going to convince you one way or another; I've worked that much out.'

'Congratulations,' she muttered, finding it hard to see the money he had settled on her and this easing of pressure in their relationship as anything else but a cop-out.

'What I suggest is that we leave the question of our marriage to one side for the moment and consider our relationship as starting the night I arrived on your doorstep.' Ross had the nerve to look amused. 'That way, I can respond to any of the accusations you hurl at me.'

Scarlett frowned, a little confused. 'What—er—sort of relationship did you have in mind? As conventional courtships go, ours has been a little sudden.'

'Not really.' The intimate knowledge in his eyes made hers slide away, her skin colouring hectically. 'We're lovers, and that's something we don't have to work on; it——'

'You don't have to elaborate,' she cut in quickly, a surge of rebellion within her wanting to refuse what he was offering but the intrusion of logic telling her that that was exactly what she had engineered.

'I don't want your money,' she asserted, topaz eyes blazing with the flames of independence. 'You can put my share in trust for Jordan. After all, he's a McQuillan by blood; I'm just——'

'More of a McQuillan than anything else.' Ross quirked an eyebrow, daring her to deny it. 'I don't think you should make any hasty decisions until you've had time to think it over. Now, shall we order?'

Scarlett agreed out of compassion for the hovering waiter rather than any real feeling of hunger. She felt too mixed up to eat the delicious concoctions on the menu. Ross was a puzzle to her. When she had refused to have anything to do with him, he had threatened her very security, pointing out that without the McQuillans' support she would be out of a home and a job. Now he seemed to be offering her considerable financial independence. It occurred to her that any legal dealings with

Ross would need fine attention to detail. No doubt the small print would stipulate access and areas of influence over Jordan's future that would replace the unspoken rights the family had negotiated in Ross's absence. Motive and counter-motive jostled for position. That Ross could be just trying to take care of his wife and son came a poor third but in truth it twanged at her conscience that she should seek out the worst interpretation of his every gesture.

The night ahead seemed alive with complications. Watching Ross as he ordered the meal, she felt the familiar stir of attraction. She admired his competence, his easy use of Portuguese, his inner confidence, and felt diminished by them at the same time. She wondered what it was that he found attractive about her. She accepted that physically he was drawn to her but he was a discerning man and presumably would want more from a deeper commitment than he would demand from a casual encounter. Her arguments inevitably led to the conclusion that this was not a relationship she could trust because she felt inadequate to deal with Ross beyond the bedroom. Despite that conviction, she had let herself be coaxed into the trip and had allowed the tug of sexual attraction to overwhelm her. Ross asked her to forget the past but Scarlett was besieged by the fear that the past had forged a blueprint for their relationship that neither of them could change.

'You've been quiet tonight,' Ross commented when they returned to their room. 'What's the matter?'

'Nothing,' she lied, eyes hectic as she made to move past him to the sanctuary of the bathroom.

'Scarlett?' He caught her wrist, staying her with easy strength. 'I know you're tired; it's been a long day. Do you want me to fix up the hammock on the balcony——?'

'I've had quite enough of hammocks, thank you.' She tried to lighten the conversation, avoiding the question he was asking.

'Scarlett.' His voice lowered, his hand lifting to frame her face. 'Will you get much sleep if I'm beside you?'

Swallowing drily, she quivered as his thumb brushed her hot cheek. Raising her lashes, she revealed unknowingly the deep confusion that tore at her. Her eyes were vulnerable but urgent with need and the message Ross received made him draw her into his arms and find her mouth with a passion as explosive as her own.

She felt his fingers smooth over her collarbone and run around the back of her neck, winnowing through her hair as his mouth fed the hunger in her, searing her mind of all doubts as to the wisdom of indulging her sensuality in his arms. Scarlett felt the heat of him engulf her, wanted the crushing demand of his mouth, her slim hips pressed into the hard planes of his, eager to have him as helpless as she.

'You're a crazy woman, do you know that?' Ross breathed into her mouth, biting her lower lip as she unconsciously tried to stop the talking. 'All night, while we're having dinner, you're saying no——' he watched her unbutton his shirt with amused indulgence, his eyes darkening when her hand slipped inside the material '—then suddenly you can't wait.'

'Can you?' The husky enquiry was muffled, Scarlett much more interested in the tactile exploration of his body, her slim fingers aware of the tightening of his diaphragm as her quest took her to the taut plane of his stomach.

'It might be an idea not to make the same mistake we did last time. I'm beginning to understand how it happened.' He pushed the strap of the green dress off one of her shoulders, caressing the golden skin, his eyes on the resentful curve of her mouth. 'A young virgin suddenly exploding in passion is enough to confuse any man, especially a man who wanted you very badly.' Ross accurately described their first sexual encounter and Scarlett shuddered at the memory.

'You told me that you wanted me and that was why you were going away.' She felt the same feeling of bewilderment and Ross gathered her to him, holding her comfortingly. 'Everyone I cared about seemed to go away; it——'

'Shush, I'm not going away.' He smoothed her forehead with his lips, his hand stroking her hair comfortingly. 'I'll look after you properly this time. Last night, we can't help.'

Scarlett didn't reveal that his consideration had been a little late last time and fate had exacted full measure. His mouth traced her cheekbone and ran down the side of her nose to the corner of her mouth, coaxing a response from her tremulous lips.

'I want what you are now.' Ross licked a path of fire across her throat. 'Not a lonely teenager. You're a woman.' He bit her gently, making Scarlett's knees quake. 'I'm going to help you cope with the fact.'

With a swift economy of movement he caught her to him and placed her on to the bed, sliding on top of her, his hands burrowing in the fire of her hair, his eyes meeting the topaz gaze with a challenge in his. 'Coping doesn't mean running away into the blaze of sex to feel guilty tomorrow, does it, Scarlett?'

'I don't know what you mean,' she denied restlessly, irritated by his insistence that they talk.

'Then why is it that this is the only way you give yourself to me?' he demanded savagely. 'The rest is a fight every inch of the way.'

It was true, she acknowledged, her lashes narrowing. But she wasn't just fighting him, she was fighting herself as well. She had loved him when he'd left her to follow Joanne and knew she was doing all that she could not to let that love into her adult life. Sensuality, she decided, was a fact of nature, ignoring the fact that so far Ross had been the only one to ignite her passion to such heights.

'We've only known each other a matter of weeks,' she reminded him breathlessly. 'Don't rush me.'

'Bitch,' he breathed on a growl of laughter. 'I should go and sleep in that hammock to teach you a lesson.' The fact that his fingers were busily undoing the buttons to her vest-dress rather argued against his stated intention. Below, she wore a strapless bra that showed the brazen peaks of her aroused nipples.

'You're far too beautiful to remain unappreciated.' He traced one hard peak with the tip of his finger, using the silk covering it to arouse her further.

Scarlett lost the sense of his words, her arms winding around his neck and urging him closer, her mouth roaming his neck and shoulders while he slowly stripped her body of clothes, his hands moving to caress the length of her back before forcing her back against the bed, twisting his hands into her hair to still her before taking her mouth in a kiss that emphasised his intention to drain everything she had to give.

The slow, suggestive push of his tongue into her mouth made Scarlett quiver with response, her whimper of pleasure bringing the increased pressure of his hips into hers. Her fingers sought his belt, feeling perspiration break out all over her body at the groan of approval that met her action.

Outside another downpour began, the atmosphere hot and sticky. Ross raised his hips so that she could push the material down over his thighs, his eyes dark as night as he watched her absorbed expression. The rain rattled against the balcony doors in violent fury as Scarlett followed her desires, using what she had learnt in their nine months of marriage to make him as unbearably aroused as she. Her red-gold hair silked around his thighs as she gave him pleasure until Ross hauled her up his body and buried himself deeply within her, his passion as raw and vital as she could have wished.

His possession was total. It resounded in every nerve in Scarlett's body. It was as if he had branded every living cell that made her a woman and completed her totally. Here in the depths of the earth's womb she felt mated in a totally primitive sense.

The slow drift back to reality was met with total enervation. Ross still covered her, his heart thudding against her breast, his face buried in her hair.

'Philip Parker must be made out of stone,' he mumbled into her ear. 'I'm glad he hasn't had you.'

'You insensitive——' Squirming from underneath him, she turned her back on him, unable to leave the bed for an imprisoning arm.

'You'll have to learn how to take a compliment.' His mouth wandered leisurely over her back, despite her stiffened shoulders. She felt him pause and kiss the small mole, shaped like a teardrop, inside her shoulderblade. She forced herself not to respond. If they made love again she would fall apart totally; her emotions thudded against the battened doors of her heart, barely contained by the defences she had so carefully constructed.

'Goodnight, sweet fantasy,' Ross's voice mocked her.

She didn't reply, staring out into the darkness, wondering how she was going to deal with the days, weeks to come. An affair in Brazil she could just about deal with but when Ross invaded her home, her very life, how would she deal with it then?

CHAPTER NINE

RIO seemed almost tame compared to the frontier town of Marabá. The hotel was the same but the honeymoon suite was booked and Ross appeared to be satisfied with new accommodation that provided two silk-covered divans. He had been immersed in the transfer arrangements for his holding in the hotel chain during the flight and Scarlett had time to think about the predicament she was in.

It was pointless to continue with the grudge against the past; Ross was right about that. They were two different people, both more mature, and she certainly wasn't the clinging vine she had been then. Ross, on the other hand, was still an unknown quantity and by his admission time would be the only proof of the steadfastness of his commitment. The idea of going back to the beginning—no, to change the beginning and actually date—was a novel one. She had dated Philip but that had been a kissing friendship. Dating Ross would mean an affair indulging the passionate attraction between them. It would certainly puzzle their family and friends but it appealed in a way that plunging into living together or deciding on divorce certainly didn't. Scarlett felt a few qualms on reaching this decision; for one thing, she always seemed to end up doing what Ross wanted, despite her misgivings. But then she was too emotionally confused to separate her warring instincts and Ross, as ever, had a way of cutting through to the crux of the thing.

Ross closed the file he had been reading with a sigh of satisfaction. 'I'm happy with the agreement; it's almost as I wanted. Would you mind dining with Adrade and his party tonight? We can plead jet-lag if it drags on.'

'No—er—fine.' She was surprised that he had asked her but then she supposed he could do no less after her complaint that he hadn't involved her in the decision about selling out his interests. It was on the tip of her tongue to ask if the lovely Maria would be there but she curbed herself just in time. If she was serious about making a new start, she would have to quell the defensive side of her nature that made her attack before she could be hurt.

'Will it be a grand affair?' she enquired, wondering if the bewitching black dress should finally get an airing.

'The Adrades tend to be flamboyant, within certain chic boundaries. They're also great gossips, so don't be surprised if they ask some awkward questions. The women are undoubtedly the worst.'

'How many of them are there?' she queried, a little bit daunted.

'You can handle it. Just imagine yourself slaying them in the mud.' He laughed at her outraged expression. 'The grapevine works fast; don't be surprised if they know about that.'

'I'm almost tempted to feign a headache.'

'Please don't.' It was simply said but she turned to look at him, laughing in surprise.

'I didn't mean it. I wouldn't miss it for the world. A night out with Brazil's high society—just think of the stories I can tell in my little café back in darkest Yorkshire.'

He smiled but when their eyes met she could tell he was relieved. It seemed that Ross wanted her along for the ride. She quelled a bubble of pleasure, not sure whether he needed her for fair means or foul. There was something about the Adrade business that wasn't quite straightforward. She mentally castigated herself for her mistrust but acknowledged that she wasn't quite ready to open herself to the pain of betrayal. Maturity brought caution and at twenty-four she felt unable to discard the lessons of the past.

The black lace dress was certainly something. It crossed over at the cleavage in loose folds, the skirt short but with overlapping tails of lace that made it look exotic and yet classy at the same time. It was a dress that suggested more than it exposed and in that achieved something unique compared to more explicit creations.

Making use of the hairdresser's, Scarlett had her hair styled so that the left side was clipped and a mane of hair cascaded over her right shoulder. The effect startled her; the contrast achieved made her look young and open to life in a way she hadn't been or felt for years. The stylist clapped her hands in delight and insisted that she be allowed to advise on cosmetics. She emerged from the salon's ministrations with a lightness in her step and an anticipation for the night ahead that surprised her.

'What do you think?' she asked Ross some time later, when she had put the finishing touches to her appearance. She found it easy to ask because the woman who twirled elegantly for his inspection was a salon creation.

Ross turned from the drinks cabinet, his eyes widening as he took in the transformation. 'I think what I know,' he purred sensuously. 'You're a very attractive woman.' His eyes lingered on the sheath of wicked lace. 'Are you dressing to please me or please yourself?'

The question surprised her but she understood it. Ross had been very critical about her appearance. He was asking if she felt comfortable with this revamped Scarlett or if she was merely conceding to his wishes.

'Does it matter?' Her eyes glittered with muted challenge.

'Perhaps you aren't ready for the question.' His expression was enigmatic. 'Do you want a drink? The car will be around the front in ten minutes.'

'No, thank you.' Scarlett felt that sobriety would help her keep her wits about her. Her emotions were rioting all over the place and alcohol would only add to the confusion she felt.

The journey to the Adrade home was a tense one. Scarlett didn't know what to expect and Ross was silent, his fingers drumming against the car door as if he was preparing himself for a confrontation.

Their arrival at the Adrades' home came as an anticlimax. It was lavish and the collection of expensive machinery in the drive suggested it was to be a large party rather than an intimate get-together.

'It looks as if half of Rio are here,' she commented lightly, finding Ross's silence unnerving.

'The expensive half,' he agreed.

The Adrades were as inquisitive as Ross had promised. Eduardo and Eva Adrade wondered over her youth and viewed the small picture she had of Jordan with interest. At first it seemed flattering but then it occurred to Scarlett that they had very carefully checked out Ross's story. It wasn't until Ross disappeared into the study with Eduardo Adrade that she had her suspicions confirmed. Maria Adrade, who had been keeping her distance, approached like a storm cloud.

'How do you like Rio, Mrs McQuillan?' She viewed Scarlett with insolent eyes. 'You are no doubt still considering your good fortune at finding your husband alive and very rich.'

Scarlett swallowed, her eyes widening with surprise. 'That's not quite how I'd put it. Naturally, everyone at home was delighted to discover Ross had survived the crash——'

Maria Adrade laughed bitterly. 'How polite you English are, so tame in your emotions. If he were my man I would have searched the jungle for him, not sat at home and waited for news.'

'Would you?' Scarlett enquired politely. Maria Adrade didn't look the type to break a nail, never mind wade into the Amazon with a young baby at her hip, which seemed to be demanded of any self-respecting wife here.

'Yes, I would. I had my flight booked to join him in England. We were to be married on his return.' Maria Adrade enjoyed the shock in her rival's eyes. 'If he hadn't conveniently produced a wife, my father would have made him sorry for betraying my love, not made him rich by buying him out!'

Scarlett was left numb, watching the other woman flounce away satisfied that she had reeked a measure of revenge for the hurt she undoubtedly felt.

'The charming Maria.' An American accent came from near by and Scarlett turned to view a tall, fair-haired man who extended his hand to her. 'I'm Troy Lyle, a friend of Chad—no, Ross's. That's kinda hard to get used to; it must be strange for him too, a whole past to re-learn.'

'My name is Scarlett.' She smiled brittly, trying to cover up her reaction to the Brazilian woman. 'My mother was a fan of *Gone with the Wind* and the hair clinched it.'

The American smiled warmly. 'It's nice. Don't take too much notice of Maria; she's spoilt and I guess she's had a little too much to drink.'

Maria Adrade hadn't seemed the least bit inebriated and Scarlett guessed that Troy Lyle was trying to smooth over the incident. She put a brave face on it but inside a host of questions were building up. Had Ross invited her to Brazil to help extricate himself from an awkward business arrangement? The embarrassment of personal involvement with his partner's daughter had been nicely side-stepped by his producing a wife. A wife who had backed up his story to the hilt and left him nothing more than a victim of circumstance.

Her eyes rested briefly on Maria Adrade and she wondered if the woman was another of Ross's casualties, serving a purpose and left behind as he moved on. She couldn't blame the woman for feeling hurt; her whole life had been turned upside-down by Ross's eventful visit to England.

'Would you like to dance?' Troy Lyle invited with a charming smile.

'Thank you.' A resurgence of pride made her accept his offer and she joined the exotic throng moving to the pulsating music.

Ross reappeared a short time later; Scarlett caught sight of him cruising around the edge of the dance-floor, stopping to talk to people here and there, looking relaxed and familiar with his environment.

She felt his approach and wasn't surprised when Troy excused himself and Ross took her into his arms. She didn't have to see the look they exchanged to know that the American's intervention hadn't been by chance.

'Enjoying yourself?' The question was asked warily.

'Very much,' she lied. 'Everything signed and sealed?'

He smiled with satisfaction. 'Yes. The end of one era, the start of another. Will you be glad to get home?'

'I've missed Jordan,' she prevaricated, not daring to think of the time ahead.

'Missed your woolly jumpers and wellingtons,' he teased, his dark eyes gleaming with laughter. 'What would they make of this exotic creature in my arms? I wonder if Jordan would recognise you?'

'Of course he would. He'd just wonder why I've got my hair done funny.' She kept up the pretence that they were spending a pleasant evening together.

'Maybe the change is just for grown-up boys.' He tightened his arms, bringing her closer to him, breathing in the scent of her hair. His lips brushed her neck and Scarlett tensed, holding her body rigid so that he wouldn't feel the shiver of response.

'Relax, we're married, remember,' he coaxed her huskily.

'I thought we were just dating, remember,' she responded smartly. 'Besides, I think it would be tactful not to rub salt in the wound, don't you?'

'Maria, you mean.' He glanced across at the woman and then back at Scarlett. 'She'll get over it. Life doesn't fulfil every whim, even if you are an Adrade.'

How could he be so heartless? Maria Adrade was baring her soul in public and Ross could just wash his hands of the woman he had been prepared to marry. His main interest appeared to her in pacifying her father rather than in any attempt to let Maria down gently.

The next hour was spent saying goodbye, as Ross said farewell to his friends. They were given several gifts and Scarlett's face ached by the time she had smiled her thanks for the umpteenth time.

Ross was expansive on the way back, telling her stories about his life in Brazil. He was a marvellous raconteur and she couldn't help laughing in parts when he admitted some of his biggest blunders and how he'd extricated himself from some hair-raising situations.

'You're certainly a survivor,' she commented when they returned to the hotel room. 'This Adrade business; am I right in thinking a long-lost wife helped you get out of a sticky situation? What would you have done if I'd refused to play along—take the family album? Not quite so effective. I know——' she pretended to be inspired '—maybe Jordan could have accompanied you on a father-and-son-get-to-know-each-other basis. I could have been explained away, suffering from a flu bug or something, and——'

'What are you talking about?' Ross bit out explosively. 'Why should I need you to sell my business? I asked you on this trip to try and break down the ice between us but you won't let that happen, will you? Your immature little mind has to leap to the next preposterous conclusion to make sure you can keep your feelings nice and safe. It would be laughable if it weren't so pathetic.'

'Pathetic!' she shrieked, her red-gold hair catching fire in the subdued wall lighting as it rippled over her shoulder. 'I'll tell you what's pathetic! Ditching a girl at the altar without a single regret, your only concern seeming to be whether you can get her father to cough up a good deal on the hotel business. How heartless can you get?'

Ross laughed cynically. 'Your faith in me is touching. Where did you hear that particular fairy-story? Maria? She has a highly developed imagination. The Adrades may have nurtured the hope that I would save them the bother of buying me out by marrying their daughter but I never made a proposal nor did more than take Maria to dinner a few times.'

Scarlett didn't believe him and her rejection was evident in her gaze. 'Then why did the family quiz me on details of our relationship, ask to see a picture of Jordan? Why did Maria tell me she was about to follow you to England when you dropped the bombshell of our marriage? Why did she tell me you were to be married on your return?'

'Why ask me?' He turned away to pour himself a drink. 'You've got all the answers.'

'I think you use everything you've got to get what you want whether it's your considerable intellectual skills, your gambling instincts or your sexuality. Yes, you're a survivor all right, without one trace of compassion for the promises you break on the way.'

'Finished?' Ross turned to face her, nursing a brandy. 'Is this a one-way character assassination or can I play too?'

'This isn't a game.' She gritted her teeth, hissing the words.

'Yes, it is. It's called insecurity and I'm getting bored playing.'

'Well, if you're bored, it's time to move on. Nice timing, Ross; you've just got out of going home and enduring being a husband and a father.'

'I intend to be a father to Jordan despite your hysterics. What I am to you remains to be seen. The only place you make sense is in bed.'

'I want to go home,' she stipulated icily. 'Right now.'

'We're booked on a plane in the morning.' He spoke as if she were addled. 'Go to bed. I won't disturb you. This nightmare can't end soon enough for me.'

With that, he turned on his heel and left the room, leaving his brandy untouched on the drinks cabinet. Scarlett stared at the door, feeling the tension flood out of her and misery take its place.

'What a mess!' She blinked back tears and crossed the room, nursing the brandy glass in her hands. She sipped the fiery liquid, the first alcoholic drink she had had that night, and considered the future. Nothing had changed, but she tried to cheer herself up. Life had been settled and comfortable before Ross had reappeared on her doorstep and it could be that way again.

Who are you kidding? she demanded savagely of herself. Without Ross her world was dried up and colourless. The shock of his disappearance had numbed her emotionally, Jordan receiving what was left of her meagre store of human feelings. Ross had brought her vibrantly alive; without him she was banished to a grey world of dissatisfaction. She recognised it, she had been through this all before, but the intensity of the pain shuddered through her, tears trickling down her cheeks to sting saltily in her nose and mouth.

A surge of rebellion rose within her. She wouldn't let him know he had hurt her again. This time she was going to leave the relationship with her head held high.

The journey back to Heathrow was passed in chilled civility. As far as Scarlett knew, Ross hadn't returned to the hotel room that night. He looked pale and tired and viewed the hostess trolley like an enemy, which made her think he'd drowned his sorrows. Good! She didn't like to think of him having an easy conscience. She determinedly concentrated on a novel she had bought at the airport and tried to act as if they had reached an amicable separation, mutually agreeing that their relationship was unworkable.

'What's the official version of our latest stand-off?' Ross queried as they circled Heathrow.

'Sorry?' She put down her book and looked at him with interest. 'You're not planning to announce it to the Press, are you?'

'Don't be irritating. I was thinking of my parents.'

'Tell them you intend to be a father to Jordan; that was what you said last night, wasn't it?'

'Scarlett——?'

'That's all you can tell them, isn't it?' She turned her head away, pretending to be interested in the lights below.

'OK. If that's the way you want it. I can see there's no persuading you from your imagined grievances.'

He sounded as if he was humouring her and Scarlett didn't like that. She had the feeling that Ross wouldn't be satisfied until he had squeezed the last ounce of feeling out of her.

Their return was marked by muted expectation. David picked them up from the Teeside airport and drove them the thirty miles or so home. Scarlett had to endure a meal and answer questions about the trip, pretending an enthusiasm she didn't feel. Finally the ordeal was over and she returned to the gatehouse with Jordan to find no peace there.

'I thought Dad would come back with us.' Jordan had a familiar stormy look about him. 'And we'd live like a real family.'

'No, darling.' Scarlett saw no point in raising his hopes. 'I like your daddy but I don't think it's a good idea if he comes to live here. He's not far away; you'll be able to see him as much as you like.'

'Grandma says he'll go away if he doesn't have a home to come back to. And this should be his home, not the farm.'

'I don't think he'll go away, not for long. He said to me that he wants to see lots of you.' She wished Mary McQuillan would remember that although children didn't always understand the full import of a situation they were inclined to latch on to the issues that concerned them.

The following days set a pattern. Jordan would go to Saxonbridge after school and Ross would spend time with him, Jordan following him around the farm like a shadow. Somehow, Ross was always absent when she arrived to pick Jordan up and she quickly concluded that he was avoiding her. She tried to tell herself that this was good but every time she arrived at Saxonbridge and found him missing she felt a distinct feeling of anticlimax.

A week passed and Scarlett found herself craving for the very sight of him. He haunted her dreams and during waking hours she felt physically deprived of him, as if he was an addiction her system refused to do without.

'I love him,' she murmured to herself as she was busy clearing a table in the café. 'What a fool you are, Scarlett McQuillan, putting yourself through this twice.'

Philip Parker called in to see her, a little encouraged by the news on the grapevine that Ross was still at the farmhouse.

'You haven't changed your mind about moving away, have you?' he asked awkwardly, taking hold of her hand as he sensed something of her misery.

'No.' She patted his hand with her own. 'I couldn't,' she replied simply.

Philip left soon after that and Scarlett didn't regret her decision. It would be unkind to offer lukewarm emotions to another man when hers were fatally tied to Ross McQuillan.

Two weeks passed without Scarlett catching more than a glimpse of Ross. The thought of seeing him became as bedevilled as his constant absence. She was satisfied with neither, tortured by both and felt she would explode with the conflict of emotions. Whatever she had felt before was tame by comparison.

Jordan lit the fuse on the dynamite, coming home one night brimming with enthusiasm for a trip to London with his father.

'Dad said I had to ask you, Mum, but I said you wouldn't mind. I can go, can't I?'

Scarlett felt her blood boil. How dared he arrange a trip with Jordan without asking her first? If she refused to let her son go, then she would be the one put in the position of spoiling their fun. If Ross was going to London, it was for only one reason. Ross had become tired of the farm and was moving back to the bright lights. He was taking Jordan along with him to salve his conscience.

Making a quick decision, she phoned Tracy and arranged for her to open the café in the morning. She would confront Ross when Jordan had gone to school.

Next day, viewing the mellow golden stone of Saxonbridge in the early morning sunshine, she wondered why she loved the place so much when it had been the backdrop to most of her most traumatic experiences. Even in explosive temper, her gaze wandered over the house lovingly, the quiet drift of sheep and the excitable barks of Drake and Karis familiar and still welcome.

She felt guilty for bringing her temper to the house and tried to moderate her feelings until she had Ross on his own.

Mary McQuillan came out into the hallway as Scarlett let herself into the farmhouse and smiled nervously, guessing from the set expression on her daughter-in-law's face that it wasn't a social visit.

'Could I see Ross?' Scarlett began, her voice measured, gathering from her mother-in-law's demeanour that her attempts to hide her feelings weren't altogether successful.

'Ross?' Mary McQuillan repeated as if playing for time. 'Well, he's just having breakfast. Would you like some?'

Scarlett shook her head, keeping a lid on her temper with difficulty, and marched resolutely towards the kitchen.

The three McQuillan men were sitting around the kitchen table in easy conversation, a conversation that stopped abruptly upon Scarlett's appearance.

'Hello, stranger,' Ross mocked her, leaning back in his chair, the only one who looked relaxed. 'Hungry?'

He meant to inflame her; it was there in his eyes, a deliberate and premeditated attempt to provoke.

'Not opening the café today?' David McQuillan tried to ease the tense atmosphere, glancing from Scarlett to his elder brother who were locked in a private battle.

'No. Unlike Ross I put personal problems in front of business transactions.' Her antagonism got the better of her; Ross knew just how to get under her skin and it was certainly working.

'Is that supposed to mean something?' Ross's voice hardened and his eyes bored into hers.

'I'll tell you exactly what it means but in private,' she stressed, perceiving how uncomfortable the conflict was for other members of the family.

'Suddenly, she can't wait to get me alone.' Ross drank his tea in a leisurely fashion, in no hurry to relinquish the breakfast-table. 'Things are looking up.'

'I doubt you'll think so.' She spoke in a smothered tone, her cheeks reddening as he continued to view her as if she was some interesting species that had the audacity to interrupt his meal.

'Ross——' John McQuillan gave his son a grunt of disapproval. 'Scarlett is obviously upset about something——'

'Scarlett works herself up into rages on a regular basis; a man's got to eat.' He unwound himself from the chair, standing up, a dark eyebrow raised in query. 'I'm expecting a call, so the study will have to do. Is that private enough for you?'

She didn't dignify his answer with a reply, her fingers flexing, itching to strangle him.

'To what do I owe this honour?' he began sarcastically. 'You'll set tongues wagging, demanding to see me on my own.'

'I haven't been avoiding *you*!' she retorted indignantly. 'You haven't been around when I came for Jordan.'

'I've been around, you just haven't bothered to pass the time of day. You could at least remind Jordan to say goodbye to me but you can't get away quick enough. I can't believe you're rushing back to see your friendly GP; that's a slow-burning fire if ever I saw one.'

It was on the tip of her tongue to say that Philip had merely called to tell her about his new job and would be leaving the area shortly.

'Philip allows me to dictate the pace of our relationship.' Giving him an insolent look, she let him make what he liked of that. 'Jordan tells me you're going to London. He came home last night with the impression he was going with you.'

'So you're turning the heat up with Parker.' Ross closed in on her, ignoring the issue of the London trip, his eyes flaring possessively. 'Watch out, he might run away. Your kind of magic has to be matched, sweetheart; you'd tear the soul out of a man.'

'I think you're confusing me with someone else. I came to talk about Jordan.' She tried to shake him off as he seized her arms.

'If you cared about Jordan, you'd fight your corner, rather than running away on any flimsy pretext.'

'I wouldn't lower myself to fight for you!' She threw the words at him, too close to depend on anything other than bitter emotions.

'Who would you fight for?' he sneered, his eyes as black as coal. 'I'm the only one who's ever touched you.'

She was on the point of saying that could change when something in his expression stopped her. Dropping her eyes, she moved restlessly in his hold and felt his fingers relax as the fury of emotions lowered to simmering-point.

'I'm going to London for a couple of days,' he explained, with an attempt to keep his tone even. 'I'll be back Monday. You can come too. I'm keeping business to a minimum.'

'Come with you?' Her eyes mirrored the rejection of the idea. The last thing she wanted was to watch Ross being reabsorbed into the glitzy media world. 'Is Joanne acting as your agent?'

'I'm meeting with my publishers. They want me to write a book about my life in Brazil. Several of the dailies want serialisation rights.'

To say Scarlett was horrified was the understatement of the year. It didn't take much imagination to predict that her private life was about to become public property.

'I forbid you to do so much as mention my name!' She grabbed his shirt-front, her topaz eyes threatening, which was ridiculous considering the size of him.

'I don't think you can forbid anything,' he pointed out coolly. 'If you come to London you could take part in the discussions. I wouldn't worry—you're hardly likely to take up much space.'

He couldn't have hurt her more if he'd slapped her face. She visibly flinched.

'No, I suppose wives are rather *passé* when it comes to selling papers. They'll be more interested in Joanne and your antics in Brazil——'

'They're more interested in my struggle to survive after the crash. I wasn't planning on a kiss-and-tell extravaganza. You're going to have to make up your mind, Scarlett, whether you want to be part of my life or whether you're going to retire to the sidelines.' Hooking his finger under her chin, he viewed the mutinous curve of her mouth, the fire in her eyes. 'If you don't come to London with me, then whatever I decide there is my business. Is that understood?'

'Are you trying to say it would make some difference if I were there?' She twisted away from him, moving back as if he physically threatened her.

'Come and see.' He neatly turned the tables. 'What have you got to lose?'

'You'll be back on Monday?'

'Yes.' His shoulders dropped defeatedly and he sighed. 'I take it Jordan can't come either.'

Scarlett hesitated. 'You've put me in an awkward position. If you'd asked me first——'

'I meant to. Jordan overheard me on the phone. He asked if he could come. Something told me you'd object, so I told him to ask you for permission. What else was I suppose to do, pretend I didn't want him along to make things easy for you?'

Scarlett felt uncomfortable. 'If you're going on a business trip——'

'I've already told you, I'd keep it to the minimum. He could watch a video for an hour. I'd be next door; there wouldn't be a problem.'

Scarlett shook her head. 'It's too soon.'

'Who for?' Ross asked softly, disappointment at being deprived of his son's company mixed with a glimmer of understanding.

'Jordan needs time to adjust——' She broke off, unwilling to draw comparisons with her own emotional instability. She left before she could say more, barely managing a 'goodbye'. Ross watched her leave but made no attempt to delay her further.

The mile between Saxonbridge and the gatehouse felt like twenty; with every step Scarlett felt as if she was leaving something dangerous and threatening behind her. But there was no feeling of relief, merely regret mixed with a terrible restlessness.

CHAPTER TEN

JEANETTE and David McQuillan arrived with Barry on Friday evening. David took the two boys to watch a science fiction film on the video back at his own house and Jeanette unfurled a bottle of wine from its wrapping and gave Scarlett a winning smile.

'I thought you might need company.'

'Thanks.' Scarlett appreciated the offer; she hadn't wanted to be alone and only Jordan's enthusiasm for the film had made her agree for him to spend the evening at his cousin's house.

Jeanette busied herself, uncorking the bottle and pouring the ruby-red wine into two glasses while Scarlett filled decorative bowls with snacks.

'I gather you're at loggerheads with Ross again,' Jeanette commented. 'Didn't you make any progress while you were away?'

Scarlett had hoped the subject would be avoided and gave a careless shrug. 'No progress, no. In fact you could say things turned full circle. I lost all the dignity I'd gained in the last six years and turned into the same emotional jelly I was when I was seventeen.'

'You don't sound like a jelly. Mary said you were in a foul mood when you dragged Ross from the breakfast-table the other day.'

'It didn't take him long to flatten me,' she reflected bitterly. 'What can you expect from a man who can charm lady luck and any other lady he cares to glance at?' She sipped her wine, catching her sister-in-law's gaze, and smiled weakly. 'Please don't feel sorry for me; I'll start to howl again.'

Jeanette looked puzzled. 'Do you still care about Ross, then? I thought you did but David said you'd refused to go to London with him so I naturally assumed——'

'Nothing much stays private in this family, does it?' Scarlett was rather surprised at Ross; he usually played his cards pretty close to his chest.

'The walls of Saxonbridge may be thick but you two yelling at each other are hard not to hear.' Jeanette chuckled at the arrested look on Scarlett's face. 'Do you love him? I'm not being nosy, I really do have a reason for asking.'

Sighing, Scarlett nodded. 'Falling in love with the same man twice, especially the same unsuitable man, has got to qualify for a particular brand of idiocy. I'd feel a fool if I had any feelings left to spare.'

Jeanette looked smug. 'I thought so. David said Philip was more your cup of tea but I've never seen you so alive in his company; you positively light up when Ross is in the room.'

'Do I?' Scarlett replied faintly.

Jeanette got up, burrowed into her capacious shoulder-bag and brought out a journal which she put in front of Scarlett.

'That belongs to Ross. It's the journal he was writing just before he went to Brazil.' She had the grace to blush. 'David went through Ross's things after the accident. He brought them home because Mary found anything to do with Ross so painful. His diaries were locked away. I didn't read that until you were away in Brazil. I know it was a terrible thing to do but I had an argument with David about the Joanne Williams business. He seemed to think you and Ross should get together for Jordan's sake and that the past didn't matter. I said that it did and that if Ross had been having an affair with Joanne when you were married he didn't deserve a second chance.' She grimaced. 'Things got a little heated and I went up into the loft, refused to let David follow me up and read the journal for the weeks just before Ross left the farm. I told David I wouldn't let you read it unless I was sure that you loved Ross; it wouldn't have been fair otherwise.' She pushed the journal towards Scarlett. 'I promised I'd give my mother a call, so I'll leave you in peace and use the extension in the kitchen.'

Scarlett looked at the journal as if it were a snake about to bite. She presumed neither Jeanette nor David would have wanted her to read it if they thought there was anything hurtful in it but the thought that she might have misjudged Ross was rather frightening.

Taking a mouthful of wine for courage, she gingerly picked up the journal. Ross's strong handwriting was immediately recognisable and she had a moment's disquiet, guessing that he wouldn't voluntarily let her into his innermost thoughts. Yet this was a Ross whom he couldn't remember so for both of them it was a link with the old Ross who couldn't speak for himself.

At first she found it difficult, but Ross had a way of writing that drew the reader in and before long she found herself in Ross's world, one of mixed loyalties and feelings of obligation. One particular passage transfixed her and she read it with a cold chill of realisation that shook her to the core of her being...

> Scarlett was a girl on the edge of womanhood whom I wasn't strong enough to leave alone. She's everything I want but not old enough to realise it; instead she grieves for not being like Joanne, who's a kingsize pain in the neck. I know Joanne has gone off on her own to cause trouble but she's bitten off more than

she can chew this time; people disappear in the Amazon and journalists are no exception...

Scarlett blinked into awareness to find Jeanette watching her with kind eyes. The journal had come to rest on her knees and she was stunned.

'I suppose I expected him to leave me.' Her voice sounded furred, as if it came from a long way off. 'My parents always had something more important to do. I wanted the security from Ross I never had from them. If he'd ever told me he loved me, I think I would have grown up more quickly...' She smiled wistfully. 'Thank you for showing me the journal.' It was hard to express how much those few lines had meant to her; she was in a limbo land where the past was being rewritten and had yet to make sense. What she did know, if only dimly, was that if the past was healed the future was still as thorny as ever.

'Will you go to London?' Jeanette asked softly, and Scarlett frowned as if the thought were a new one.

'I don't know.' Her mind skittered over the possibility. 'I've told Jordan I couldn't get away...'

'So, you've been able to change your plans. Jordan won't ask too many questions. He wants to go. Ross is worth fighting for, Scarlett. Even if it doesn't work out at least you'd know you've done your best. You love the man, you said so—you simply have to go!'

Scarlett was still considering these words early Saturday morning as the train pulled out of York station. Jordan was sitting beside her, excited by the prospect of meeting up with Ross in London. She had meant to call Ross and advise him of their arrival but had been unable to summon up the courage to negotiate a telephone conversation. She needed to see him face to face.

The Barchester hotel was a grand affair and she explained her wish to surprise her husband and was allowed into the suite. Ross, she was informed, was dining in the restaurant.

'Can we get something to eat, Mum? I'm starving.' Jordan, oblivious to Scarlett's growing trepidation, was keen to join his father at the table.

Scarlett's back stiffened as she saw Joanne Williams at the table in close conversation with Ross. Jealousy swamped her and for a moment her eyes took fire and her nostrils flared, every inch the feline on the attack.

They both looked up at the same time, Ross looking startled, Joanne faintly embarrassed.

'Dad!' Jordan broke up the electric atmosphere, flinging himself into Ross's arms and telling him excitedly about the journey.

'Scarlett,' Ross acknowledged her over the top of Jordan's head. 'What a pleasant surprise. Won't you join us?'

The last thing Scarlett wanted to do was break bread with Joanne Williams but she found the prospect of subjecting Jordan to a scene untenable. Her own instincts were to call him every kind of louse. It took considerable self-control to allow the waiter to seat her.

'I thought you were meeting with your publisher,' she began tentatively. 'You didn't mention Joanne.'

'She's staying at the Barchester,' Ross replied blandly, and giving Jordan a menu, he pointed out the things that weren't too spicy.

'What a coincidence.' Scarlett was positively brittle.

'It's a popular hotel,' Joanne demurred. 'Ross didn't say you were to join him.'

'Impulse.' Scarlett smiled thinly. 'He was so insistent, I felt mean putting my business first, so I relented.'

Ross seemed completely at ease, his gaze speculative as if he was well aware of her discomfort. Scarlett met his eyes with deep disappointment in her own. How could he invite her to come to London with him and then when she refused turn to Joanne?

'We can go to the National History Museum, can't we, Dad?' Jordan was all enthusiasm. 'Do they have burgers here?'

'It's not McDonald's.' Scarlett laughed with forced cheerfulness. Pride made her refuse to crawl away into the shadows. 'Darling, will you be able to get another room for Jordan?'

'I don't think that will be too difficult.' A gleam of malicious humour entered Ross's dark eyes. 'I'm allowed to economise on you, I take it?'

Scarlett sent him a guileless look of non-comprehension. Joanne glanced up from the table with a relieved smile as another man joined them.

'John, I wondered where you'd got to. Let me introduce you; this is Scarlett McQuillan and Jordan, Ross's wife and son. Er—this is my fiancé, John Scott.'

Scarlett shook hands with a feeling of bewilderment. Joanne engaged! Ross appeared quite happy with the arrangement and indeed was enjoying her confusion.

'It's a bit hush-hush,' Joanne explained hastily. 'John is very popular with the teenage market——'

'Yes, I recognise him. Jordan watches the show.' It was a cops and robbers programme that was currently very successful. There was no scarcity of conversation, Jordan monopolising his TV hero while Scarlett reflected on her own shortcomings. Joanne's appearance was an unlucky coincidence but her lack of trust in Ross showed that six years hadn't matured her in that respect. Ross was really going to lap it up when she gave him the journal. Her life wouldn't be worth living.

'Lawrence Hartman is coming to the hotel this afternoon. That's off the record, Joanne.' Ross was firm and the journalist nodded.

'I promise. It sounds like an interesting story.' Her smile was weak and Scarlett scented a mystery.

'That remains to be seen. I haven't written much over the past six years; I might have lost my touch.'

'I should think it's like riding a bicycle.' John Scott was the only one unaware of the undercurrents present in the room. 'Are you going back on the box? It's best to strike while you're high profile.'

'Scarlett doesn't want to share me with a host of female fans.' Ross's expression was positively sharkish. 'She wants to lock me up and throw away the key.'

'Hardly surprising; I've just got you back,' Scarlett asserted. 'I'm sure I'll mellow given time.'

'Really?' He lifted his glass to her, in a gesture that looked like teasing mockery but she knew it was real enough.

The meal seemed to last forever. Ross played host, his mood expansive, warmth wrapping around Jordan and seemingly extended to Scarlett as well. Only she was aware of his reservations, his suspicion about her motives. In the short time they had been together, he had had reason to mistrust her consistency in the same way she had doubted his.

After lunch, Scarlett changed out of her travelling clothes, which felt rumpled, and chose a longline fluted blouse with plissé collar in cream crêpe de Chine and a multi-coloured skirt in raw silk. She was reprieved momentarily from Ross's attention by Jordan. He refused to leave them alone together, clearly enjoying the novelty of the family unit. She was dreading the explanations she would have to give and didn't find Ross's attitude very encouraging.

Fastening her pearl drop earrings, she viewed her appearance, aware of the sudden taste for soft, seductive materials, enjoying the fragile glitter of jewellery, reflecting that practicality had been relegated down her list of priorities.

'Mirror, mirror...' The soft taunt wasn't without a hint of admiration and she straightened her shoulders and turned, unconscious challenge in the tilt of her chin as she walked towards the door Ross held open for her.

The meeting with Lawrence Hartman was businesslike and to the point. Ross maintained that he wished to begin the book with his first memory after the crash. When Hartman speculated on the use of family memories and Press cuttings he refused.

Scarlett felt some of the tensions ease away. Her worst fears were not to be realised. When Ross wouldn't be persuaded she recognised both strength and integrity and wondered at her own blind prejudice. In his days as a reporter, Ross had always been known for his hard work, uncompromising style and yet she had wilfully tarred him with instincts that marked the hyenas of the trade.

'The book starts there or not at all.'

'And where does it finish?' the publisher queried. 'Here?'

Ross glanced at his wife. 'When I write the final chapter.'

'I'm sure you know you can dictate your own terms, Ross. What sort of timetable have you got?'

'Initially six articles for the Sunday market, in the next two months, and then I'll expand on that.'

The rest of the meeting involved financial details. Ross, she sensed, was more interested in establishing himself in the present than making money, especially since he had a considerable fortune behind him from the sale of the hotels.

'Heady stuff,' Ross commented drily on the meeting as they rescued Jordan from a Disney video and set out for the promised museum visit.

Scarlett was surprised how much she enjoyed the day. Ross was genuinely fascinated by the museum and she watched him run through some of the teaching models with Jordan, their dark heads bent over one of the displays, both absorbed. They had huge ice-creams in an American burger bar and arrived back at the hotel at seven o'clock. Ross had swapped his room for one with an adjoining bedroom for Jordan.

Running a bath for her son, Scarlett saw that he had everything he needed, leaving the door slightly ajar before going back into the main room.

'I must admit to being eaten up by curiosity.' Ross spoke in an undertone, watching her as she took the journal out of her suitcase. 'What's that?'

'Your journal.' She swallowed drily. 'I—I owe you an apology. I wouldn't have read it but Jeanette seemed to think it was important that I did.'

Approaching her, he looked at the journal but refused to take it. 'What does it say? Dear Scarlett, don't jump to conclusions?'

'Read it.' She pushed it towards him a little desperately and he winced as it jabbed his stomach.

All the time she was taking out Jordan's pyjamas and making sure he had washed behind his ears she could hear him flicking through the pages, conscious of the occasional pause and his glance on her heated profile.

He didn't speak and she took Jordan to bed, telling him a story and lying beside him until his dark lashes drifted down on to his cheeks.

'It's been a smashing day, Mum,' he murmured before his breathing evened out, and she smiled, doubting it would go down as a smashing day for her.

It took a lot of courage to go out and face Ross. When she did, she could tell it wasn't going to be easy. He looked fairly bloody-minded.

'I now understand the tepid apology.' Dark eyes raked her mercilessly. 'It has to be written in blood before you can absolve me of cheating you. I thought you'd actually decided to give up your grievances and come here. I must have been crazy! You don't like it, do you? You'd rather hold on to all those prejudices you've nursed over the years. Jeanette didn't do you much of a favour, did she?'

Scarlett went white. 'I didn't want to think badly of you. I loved you, Ross! If I hadn't felt furious with you for leaving I don't think I could have got through those months alone.'

'You may have survived but as far as your emotional maturity is concerned nothing much has changed. If Jordan hadn't been there today you would have left before you'd said hello; I saw the expression on your face. Despite being cleared by my journal of your juvenile accusations, you were still willing to think the worst of me, weren't you?'

'Oh, excuse me!' Scarlett felt her temper ignite. 'Every time I turn around there's some female at your heels, some lonely heart following you around.'

'I've seen Joanne twice, for the purpose of discovering what you couldn't tell me.' His gaze battled with hers. 'She was as keen to keep the past under wraps as you are. It wouldn't do her career much good if it were known that I risked my life getting her out of the mess she'd got herself into because having her boyfriend pinched by a teenager had made her behave rashly. We were supposed to cover that assignment together. It got scrapped because I didn't think it was fair to keep on working with Joanne. That's why I went to help her; she admitted that to me herself.'

Scarlett hugged her arms to her body, feeling shaken by the waves of emotion sweeping through the room. 'It's a pity Joanne never told me. I suppose she kept up that public vigil because she felt guilty but it made me feel as if I didn't count, as if I'd lost even your memory. I hated her and I hated you,' she recounted bitterly.

'At least you didn't waste your life worshipping at my shrine. I think I was your idol, not a real man you loved. I don't think you knew me at all.'

'That's a terrible thing to say!' Scarlett's mouth shook, her eyes wounded.

'Is it? Well, for someone who knows me as well as you think you do, you've missed something quite vital. Still, with your talent for fantasy, I dare say the truth is rather boring.' Picking up his jacket, he threw the key across to her. 'I'll stay at another hotel and be back for breakfast.'

For a moment, she just stared at the key. Then with sudden decision she flew across the room and stood in front of the door, her hands pressed against his chest. If he chose to thrust her out of the way, it would be an uneven battle, but if determination counted for anything Scarlett would put up a good fight.

'I don't want you to go, Ross.' Taking a deep breath, she lifted her gaze to his, her eyes passionate with intensity. 'Please don't go. I can't—I don't want to live without you any more.'

There was a silence when his gaze absorbed hers into a world of black torment, his breath harsh, her fingertips conscious of the thudding of his heart and the movement of his chest.

'Why?' he demanded harshly. 'Life isn't very comfortable with me around, is it?'

'Comfort is overrated.' She tried to lighten the atmosphere, tears glittering in her eyes as she gave a choked laugh. 'You make me angry and you make me cry. You bring love and passion and beside that everything else is grey.'

'Grey?'

'Very grey.'

The black torment had mellowed to something more potent, something infinitely sensual, like storm clouds magically transformed into a velvety evening sky.

'I can't remember Joanne. I don't know whether I cheated on you or not. All I know is that you're in my heart and soul and no other woman touches you.'

Scarlett drowned in the depths of his eyes. It was time to trust this man of hers. She was no longer a teenager, hurt by parental negligence, she was a full-blooded woman who could fight her corner and give as passionately as she took.

'I accept that.' Her mouth trembled with feeling.

'My world was a world of ashes.' Ross spoke softly, his hands framing her face. 'With dreams so vivid that they robbed the world of colour. You've haunted me, Scarlett McQuillan; you're the woman I can't get past. I crossed continents to find you, and when I did you screamed at me like a banshee.'

'I'm sorry,' Scarlett whispered against his lips and their mouths fused in a warm kiss that escalated into a quickly burning fire.

'I don't want you to be sorry,' he breathed into her mouth. 'Just to love me.'

'I do.' She kissed him feverishly. 'I love you so much.' Scarlett felt the heavy burden of restraining her feelings lift and laughed breathlessly as his mouth moved down over her chin and he kissed the delicate gold skin at the base of her throat.

'It's been awful trying to pretend I didn't care about you,' she admitted, shivering with delight as he nuzzled the join of her neck. 'Did you really remember me?'

'No. It's a line I use to get women into bed. What do you think?' He lifted his head, his dark eyes chiding the slight doubt that lingered behind the joy. 'When I first saw you, there was this feeling of familiarity. I had these dreams——' He grinned at the heat that flooded her cheeks. 'I knew somewhere there was someone who had been very special to me. Sometimes I used to wake up, soaked in sweat, absolutely terrified, with a terrible feeling of loss. When I found out there was a place called Saxonbridge I had to come and see if there was anything here for me. Despite the storm, that night I found you, I couldn't go away and wait until morning; I had to know. Something told me I'd found the right place.'

'I didn't give you much of a welcome,' Scarlett murmured, bending her head, feeling she had made a lot of mistakes.

'No,' he agreed but his voice was teasing. 'Even if the matter of Joanne hadn't been between us, you were right to protect Jordan.' Hooking a finger under her chin, he took in the emotional heat in her eyes and the soft glisten of her lips with an intensity that raised the sexual tension between them.

'I loved you in my dreams and fell in love with you all over again.' Watching the tell-tale flicker of her lashes, he smiled, his free hand brushing her hair away from her profile. 'Even when you were spitting fury at me, all I could think of was how magnificent you looked.'

'You said I was a frump,' she reminded him with a hint of her old fire. 'Do you still think that, Ross?' She teased his lapel with her thumb and index finger.

'I wouldn't dare.' Amused, he ran his fingers under her hair, satisfied at the appreciative movement of her head that encouraged his touch.

'Is Jordan a heavy sleeper?'

'Reasonably.' She gazed up at him limpidly. 'Why, frightened you snore?'

'What an unromantic little soul you are,' he berated her, lifting her off her feet and whirling her around until she begged him to stop. Laughing, he obliged, placing her on the bed with roguish determination. 'You can wear what you like during the day, as long as you promise to wear nothing at all when you come to bed.'

'I think that can be arranged.' She smiled meltingly at him and his dark features lost all trace of humour, becoming seriously intent. Undoing his shirt, he came towards the bed, the white cotton falling away to reveal the masculine brawn of his chest, his skin almost bronze in the subdued lamplight.

Scarlett quivered as he slid on to the bed beside her, taking in his scent with her breath, a heavy languidness seeping through her limbs which she knew would turn into a restless ache before he gave her release.

'I'm going to be the only man in your life, do you understand that?' His finger traced the fragile line of her jaw.

'Yes, I know,' she promised quietly. 'There has never been anyone else.'

'Good.' His mouth played with hers with an erotic lack of pressure. 'And you're changing your GP.'

'Philip never was my GP. He's leaving for the south, anyway,' she whispered between kisses.

'I have a few demands of my own,' she murmured moments later as his fingers dispensed with the small pearly buttons on her blouse. Her tawny eyes narrowed as fiery shivers chased over skin when he stroked the blouse down over her shoulders. 'But I think they can wait.'

'I think so too.' Ross's voice was thick with wanting, his mouth taking hers in a kiss of soul-aching sweetness. Words were lost between them as their passion became incandescent, both wanting the glorious insanity that bonded them in the flesh to honour the words they had spoken.

Nearly a year later, Scarlett slowly approached the small hill that had witnessed her passionate initiation, biting her lip and viewing Ross as he sat in the sun's dying light, staring out over the sea. She had known for a while that he was beginning to claw back pieces of the past, and was unable to imagine how frustrating it must be to have memories surface, some making sense, others adrift, the sense of them still trapped in darkness.

Joining him, she sat down, aware of the slight movement of his head to acknowledge her. It wasn't necessary; she knew he had sensed her long before she reached him. It was like that between them, a feeling of completion when the other was near. Scarlett had become confident in his love, enough to give him room to breathe and follow his own path.

'I was a selfish, opinionated bastard,' he bit out angrily. 'I don't know how you could forgive me. I thought you were too young to feel anything that would last. I was too busy protecting my feelings to consider yours.'

'It's not unusual to fall in and out of love at seventeen,' she considered evenly. 'It wasn't an easy situation, considering I was living at Saxonbridge——'

'Don't pretend it's OK, it isn't. I should never have touched you. You were in my family's care and all I could think about was what I wanted.'

'You did intend to put some distance between us,' she pointed out in his favour. 'I couldn't bear the thought of you going and I threw myself at you.' She smiled at the memory. 'Anyway, if you changed the past, we wouldn't have Jordan and maybe we wouldn't have each other.'

Ross relaxed fractionally. 'I don't deserve you.'

Scarlett chuckled. 'I don't deserve you, but if we all got what we deserved the world might be a bit boring, don't you think?'

Ross turned to look at her, his dark eyes caressing. 'Joanne was no contest, by the way. It was finished before we made love. The assignment in Brazil was very prestigious and when I pulled out they threatened to give it to another team. Joanne tried to force the issue by going it alone, hoping I'd follow out of a sense of obligation. She was held prisoner at a small goldmine being shut down by the government because it was in a particularly sensitive area. They felt they were being unfairly discriminated against and wanted publicity for their cause. They weren't particularly worried how they got it.' His eyes pleaded for her understanding. 'You've been out there, you know what it could be like for a woman without someone who knows the ropes.' She nodded and he went on.

'When I had negotiated her freedom, I told her what I thought of her and got the first ride I could out of the area. She expected me to cut my losses and finish the assignment. It might have been better if I had.'

Scarlett shook her head with cynical humour. 'I bet she had some bad moments imagining you were going to reveal all when you came back.'

'I would imagine that's why she came up north to see me. She was testing the water, finding out how much I could remember. It wouldn't make pretty reading in the Press and her career would have sunk without a trace.'

Scarlett linked her arms around his waist, her cheek rubbing against his shoulder. 'I don't care about Joanne any more. Let her keep her career. She can't have been very comfortable these last six years thinking she was responsible for your disappearance.'

'I think you're the loveliest woman I've ever met,' Ross told her deeply.

'Come back home and tell me that,' she offered, urging him to his feet.

'What, when we've got a glorious sunset and a romantic location?'

Scarlett pouted up at him. 'I prefer a warm shower, silk sheets, a distinct lack of thistles——'

Ross gave a low, gravelly laugh. 'What happened to that impetuous seventeen-year-old?' he queried huskily.

'She grew up,' Scarlett informed him seriously, rising up on her tiptoes and kissing him tenderly. 'And,' she said, 'I'm rather glad she did.'

Hugging her to his side, his dark eyes warm with love, Ross said that he was rather glad too.

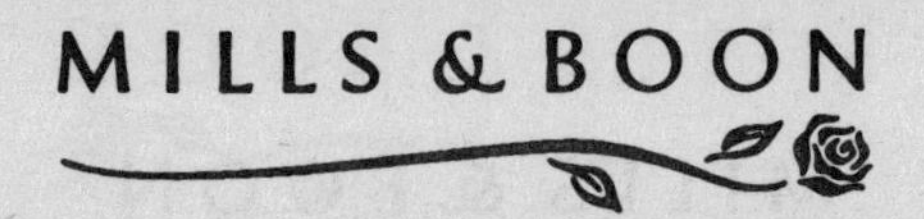

HEARTS OF FIRE by Miranda Lee

Welcome to our compelling family saga set in the glamorous world of opal dealing in Australia. Laden with dark secrets, forbidden desires and scandalous discoveries, **Hearts of Fire** unfolds over a series of 6 books, but each book also features a passionate romance with a happy ending and can be read independently.

Book 1: SEDUCTION & SACRIFICE

Published: April 1994 *FREE* with Book 2

WATCH OUT for **special** promotions!

Lenore had loved Zachary Marsden secretly for years. Loyal, handsome and protective, Zachary was the perfect husband. Only Zachary would never leave his wife...would he?

Book 2: DESIRE & DECEPTION

Published: April 1994 Price £2.50

Jade had a name for Kyle Armstrong: *Mr Cool*. He was the new marketing manager at Whitmore Opals—the job *she* coveted. However, the more she tried to hate this usurper, the more she found him attractive...

Book 3: PASSION & THE PAST

Published: May 1994 Price £2.50

Melanie was intensely attracted to Royce Grantham—which shocked her! She'd been so sure after the tragic end of her marriage that she would never feel for any man again. How strong was her resolve not to repeat past mistakes?

Next Month's Romances

Each month you can choose from a wide variety of romance with Mills & Boon. Below are the new titles to look out for next month, why not ask either Mills & Boon Reader Service or your Newsagent to reserve you a copy of the titles you want to buy – just tick the titles you would like and either post to Reader Service or take it to any Newsagent and ask them to order your books.

Please save me the following titles:	Please tick	✓
PASSIONATE OPPONENT	Jenny Cartwright	
AN IMPOSSIBLE DREAM	Emma Darcy	
SHATTERED WEDDING	Elizabeth Duke	
A STRANGER'S KISS	Liz Fielding	
THE FURY OF LOVE	Natalie Fox	
THE LAST ILLUSION	Diana Hamilton	
DANGEROUS DESIRE	Sarah Holland	
STEPHANIE	Debbie Macomber	
BITTER MEMORIES	Margaret Mayo	
A TASTE OF PASSION	Kristy McCallum	
PHANTOM LOVER	Susan Napier	
WEDDING BELLS FOR BEATRICE	Betty Neels	
DARK VICTORY	Elizabeth Oldfield	
LOVE'S STING	Catherine Spencer	
CHASE A DREAM	Jennifer Taylor	
EDGE OF DANGER	Patricia Wilson	

If you would like to order these books in addition to your regular subscription from Mills & Boon Reader Service please send £1.90 per title to: Mills & Boon Reader Service, Freepost, P.O. Box 236, Croydon, Surrey, CR9 9EL, quote your Subscriber No:................................ (if applicable) and complete the name and address details below. Alternatively, these books are available from many local Newsagents including W H Smith, J Menzies, Martins and other paperback stockists from 8 July 1994.

Name:...

Address:..

....Post Code:.........................

To Retailer: If you would like to stock M&B books please contact your regular book/magazine wholesaler for details.

You may be mailed with offers from other reputable companies as a result of this application. If you would rather not take advantage of these opportunities please tick box. ☐